PAPERCUTZ SLICES

THE FARTING DEAD

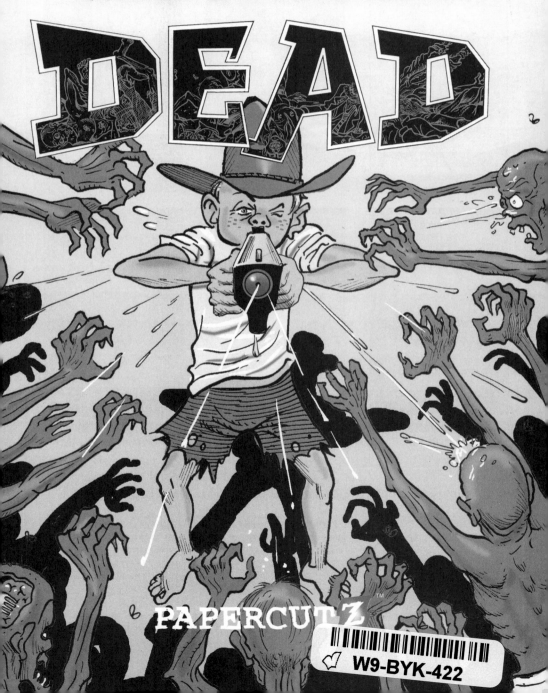

PAPERCUTZ

PAPERCUTZ™ SLICES

Graphic Novels Available from PAPERCUTZ™ (Who else..?!)

PAPERCUTZ SLICES
AN ALL-NEW, UNAUTHORIZED PARODY!
Harry Potty
AND THE DEATHLY BORING
STEFAN PETRUCHA
RICK PARKER
PAPERCUTZ

Graphic Novel #1
"Harry Potty and the Deathly Boring"

PAPERCUTZ SLICES
AN ALL-NEW, UNAUTHORIZED PARODY
breaking down
STEFAN PETRUCHA & RICK PARKER
PAPERCUTZ

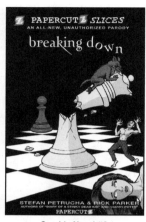

Graphic Novel #2
"breaking down"

PAPERCUTZ SLICES
PERCY JERKSON
& THE OVOLACTOVEGETARIANS
PAPERCUTZ

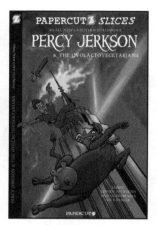

Graphic Novel #3
"Percy Jerkson & The Ovolactovegetarians"

PAPERCUTZ SLICES
AN ALL-NEW UNAUTHORIZED PARODY
THE HUNGER PAINS
Stefan
PETRUCHA
Rick
PARKER
PAPERCUTZ

Graphic Novel #4
"The Hunger Pains"

PAPERCUTZ SLICES
ONCE THEY STROVE FOR ART AND BEAUTY, AND NOW...
THE FARTING DEAD
PULL MY FINGER
PAPERCUTZ

Graphic Novel #5
"The Farting Dead"

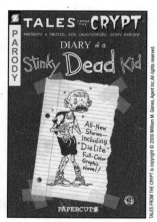

TALES FROM THE CRYPT
PARODY
PRESENTS A TWISTED, SICK, UNAUTHORIZED, GOOFY PARODY!
DIARY of a
Stinky Dead Kid
All-New Stories-- including "Die Lite" Full-Color Graphic Novel!
PAPERCUTZ

TALES FROM THE CRYPT #8
"Diary of a Stinky Dead Kid"

NEW! PAPERCUTZ™ SLICES is now available wherever e-books are sold!
Now you can read PAPERCUTZ SLICES and look like you're conducting serious business!

PAPERCUTZ SLICES and TALES FROM THE CRYPT graphic novels, the print editions, are still available at booksellers everywhere. At bookstores, comicbook stores, online, out of the trunk of Rick Parker's car, and who knows where else? If you still are unable to find PAPERCUTZ SLICES (probably because it sold out) you can always order directly from Papercutz—but it'll cost you! PAPERCUTZ SLICES is available in paperback for $6.99 each; in hardcover for $10.99 each except #5, $7.99PB, $11.99HC. TALES FROM THE CRYPT #8 is available in paperback for $7.95, and hardcover for $12.95. But that's not the worst part-- please add $4.00 for postage and handling for the first book, and add $1.00 for each additional book. Going to your favorite bookseller, buying online, or even getting a copy from your local library doesn't seem so bad now, does it? But if you still insist on ordering from Papercutz, and just to make everything just a little bit more complicated, please make your check payable to NBM Publishing. Don't ask why—it's just how it works. Send to: Papercutz, 160 Broadway, Suite 700, East Wing, New York, NY 10038
Or call 800 886 1223 (9-6 EST M-F) MC-Visa-Amex accepted

www.papercutz.com

PAPERCUTZ SLICES

#5 THE FARTING DEAD

Stefan
PETRUCHA
Writer

Rick
PARKER
Artist

PAPERCUTZ
New York

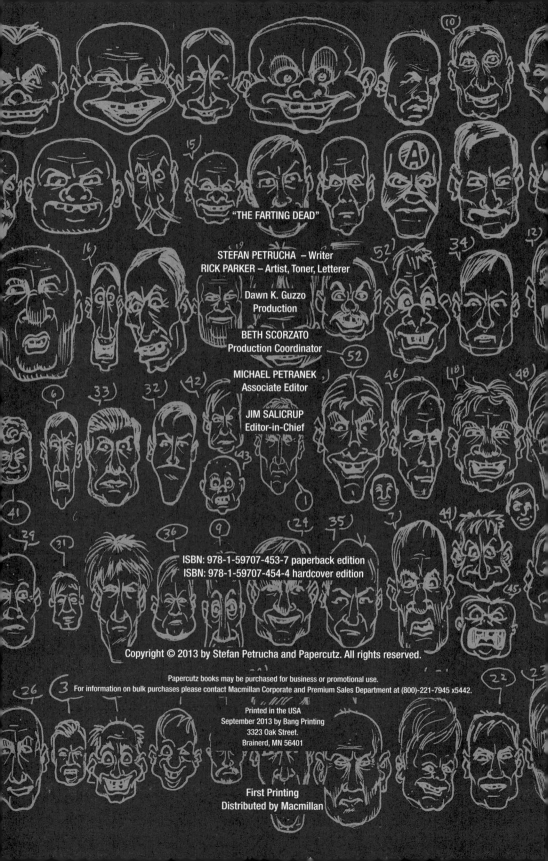

"THE FARTING DEAD"

STEFAN PETRUCHA – Writer
RICK PARKER – Artist, Toner, Letterer

Dawn K. Guzzo
Production

BETH SCORZATO
Production Coordinator

MICHAEL PETRANEK
Associate Editor

JIM SALICRUP
Editor-in-Chief

ISBN: 978-1-59707-453-7 paperback edition
ISBN: 978-1-59707-454-4 hardcover edition

Papercutz books may be purchased for business or promotional use.
For information on bulk purchases please contact Macmillan Corporate and Premium Sales Department at (800)-221-7945 x5442.

Printed in the USA
September 2013 by Bang Printing
3323 Oak Street.
Brainerd, MN 56401

First Printing
Distributed by Macmillan

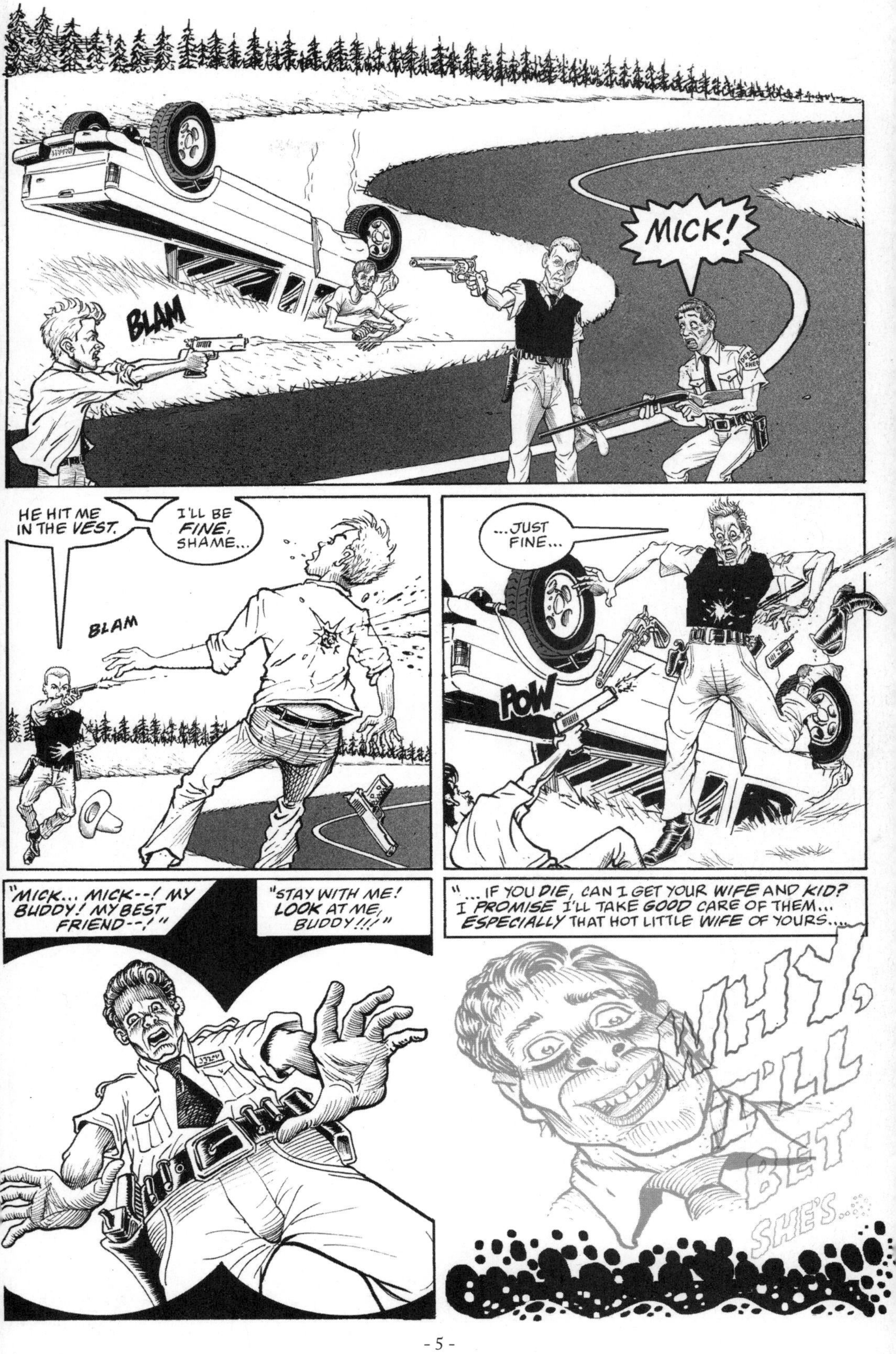
MICK!
BLAM
HE HIT ME IN THE VEST.
I'LL BE FINE, SHAME...
BLAM
...JUST FINE...
POW
"MICK... MICK--! MY BUDDY! MY BEST FRIEND--!"
"STAY WITH ME! LOOK AT ME, BUDDY!!!"
"...IF YOU DIE, CAN I GET YOUR WIFE AND KID? I PROMISE I'LL TAKE GOOD CARE OF THEM... ESPECIALLY THAT HOT LITTLE WIFE OF YOURS...
WHY, I'LL BET SHE'S...

28 DAYS LATER....

...NURSE...?

ANYONE--!??

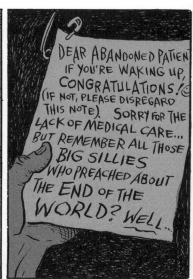

DEAR ABANDONED PATIEN
IF YOU'RE WAKING UP,
CONGRATULATIONS!
(IF NOT, PLEASE DISREGARD
THIS NOTE). SORRY FOR THE
LACK OF MEDICAL CARE...
BUT REMEMBER ALL THOSE
BIG SILLIES
WHO PREACHED ABOUT
THE END OF THE
WORLD? WELL..

HELLO...?

ISN'T THIS JUST LIKE 28 DAYS LATER? ONLY THEY'RE NOT SICK LIKE WUSSY ZOMBIES... THEY ARE REALLY DEAT!

"I DIDN'T KNOW WHAT WAS GOING ON..."

FIRE ALARM

BREAK GLASS AND RUN LIKE HELL

EXIT

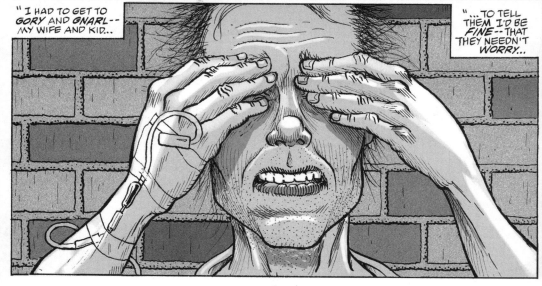

"I HAD TO GET TO GORY AND GNARL-- MY WIFE AND KID...

"...TO TELL THEM I'D BE FINE-- THAT THEY NEEDN'T WORRY...

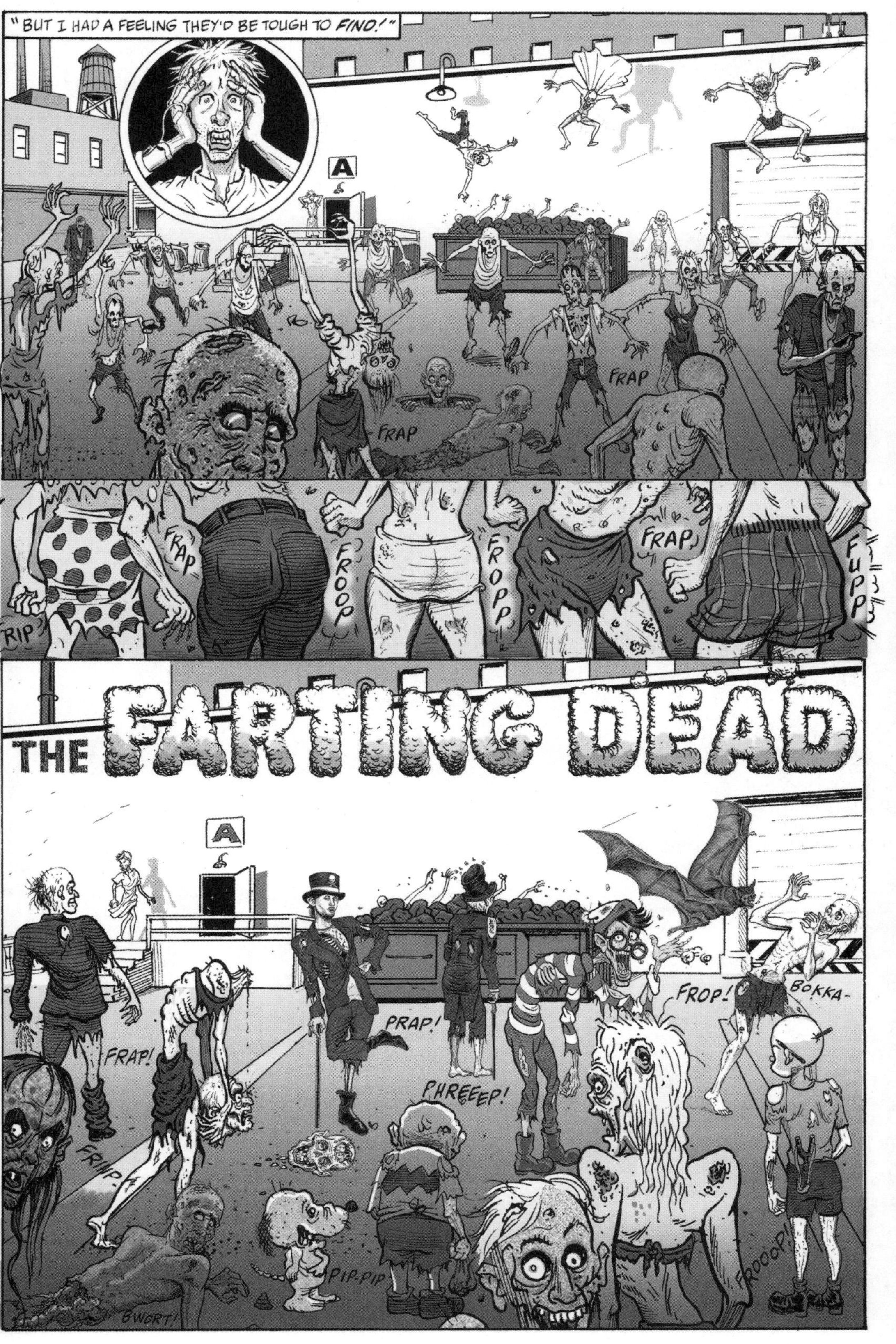
"BUT I HAD A FEELING THEY'D BE TOUGH TO FIND!"
A
FRAP
FRAP
RIP
FRAP
FROOP
FROPP
FRAP
FUPP
THE FARTING DEAD
A
PRAP!
FROP!
BOKKA-
FRAP!
PHREEEP!
FRIMP
PIP-PIP
FROOOP!
BWORT!

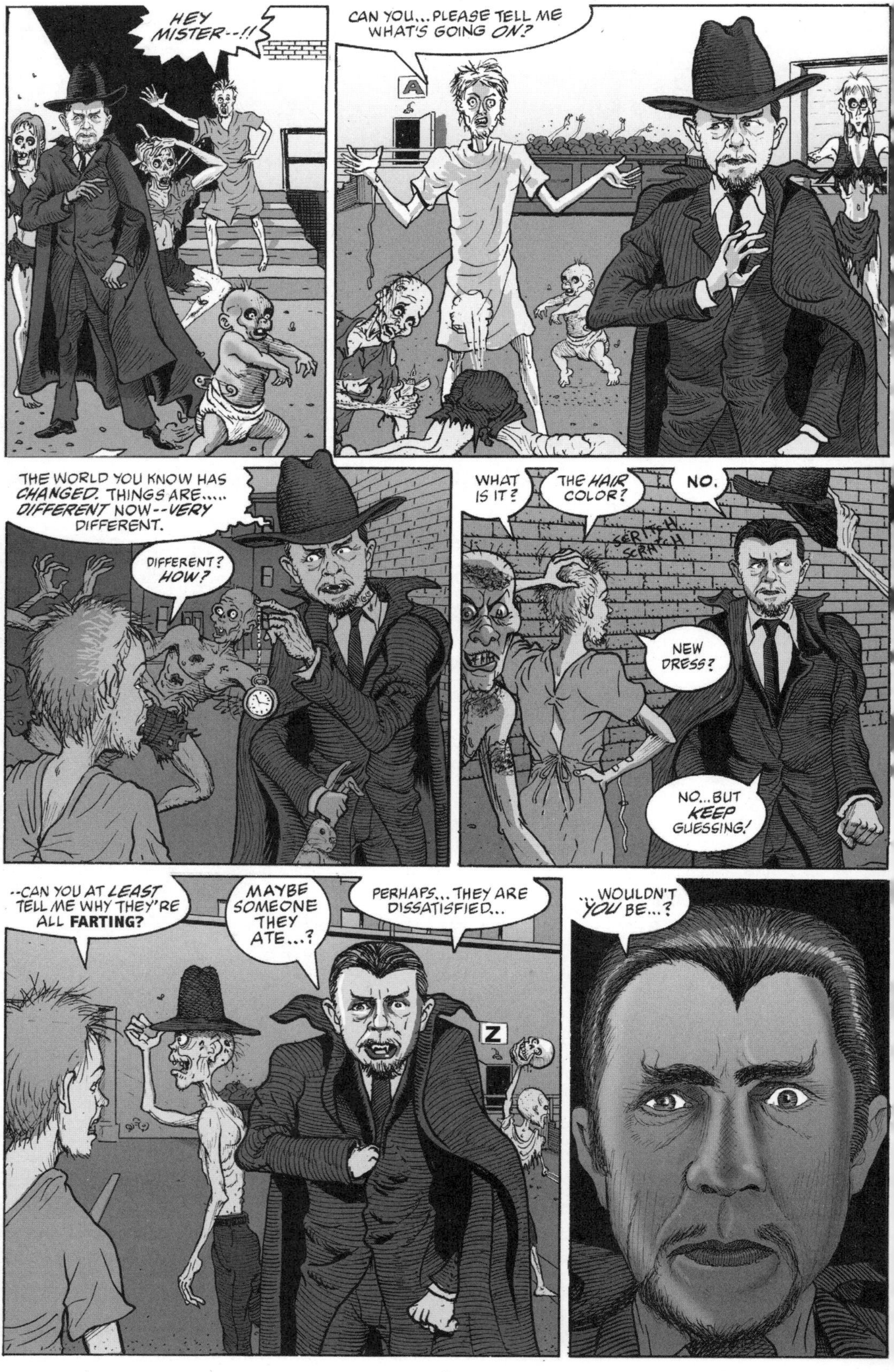
HEY MISTER--!!
CAN YOU...PLEASE TELL ME WHAT'S GOING ON?
A
THE WORLD YOU KNOW HAS CHANGED. THINGS ARE..... DIFFERENT NOW--VERY DIFFERENT.
DIFFERENT? HOW?
WHAT IS IT?
THE HAIR COLOR?
NO.
SCRITCH SCRATCH
NEW DRESS?
NO...BUT KEEP GUESSING!
--CAN YOU AT LEAST TELL ME WHY THEY'RE ALL FARTING?
MAYBE SOMEONE THEY ATE...?
PERHAPS... THEY ARE DISSATISFIED...
Z
...WOULDN'T YOU BE...?

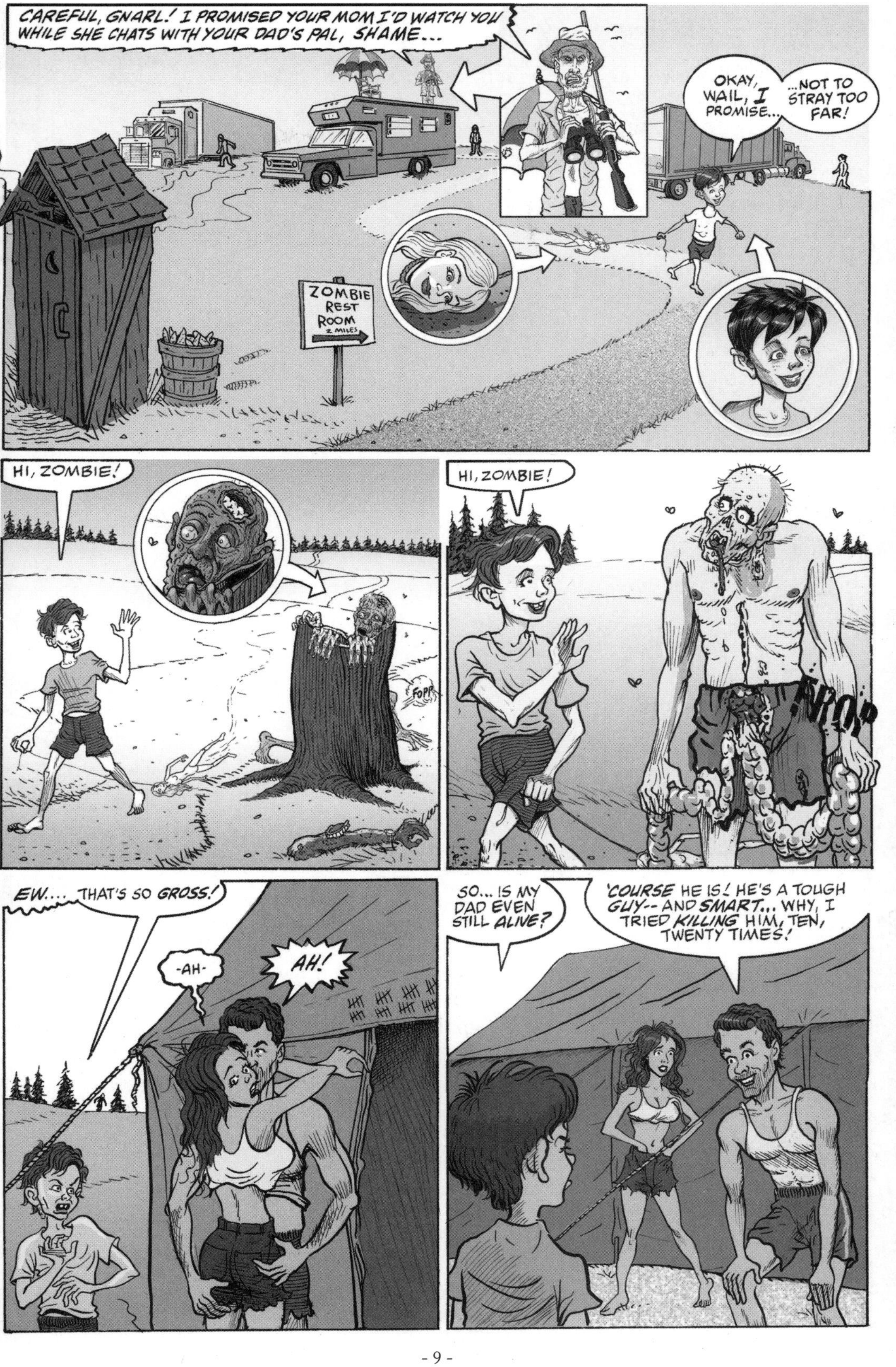
CAREFUL, GNARL! I PROMISED YOUR MOM I'D WATCH YOU WHILE SHE CHATS WITH YOUR DAD'S PAL, SHAME...
OKAY, WAIL, I PROMISE...
...NOT TO STRAY TOO FAR!
ZOMBIE REST ROOM 2 MILES
HI, ZOMBIE!
FOPP
HI, ZOMBIE!
EW.... THAT'S SO GROSS!
-AH-
AH!
SO... IS MY DAD EVEN STILL ALIVE?
'COURSE HE IS! HE'S A TOUGH GUY-- AND SMART... WHY, I TRIED KILLING HIM, TEN, TWENTY TIMES!

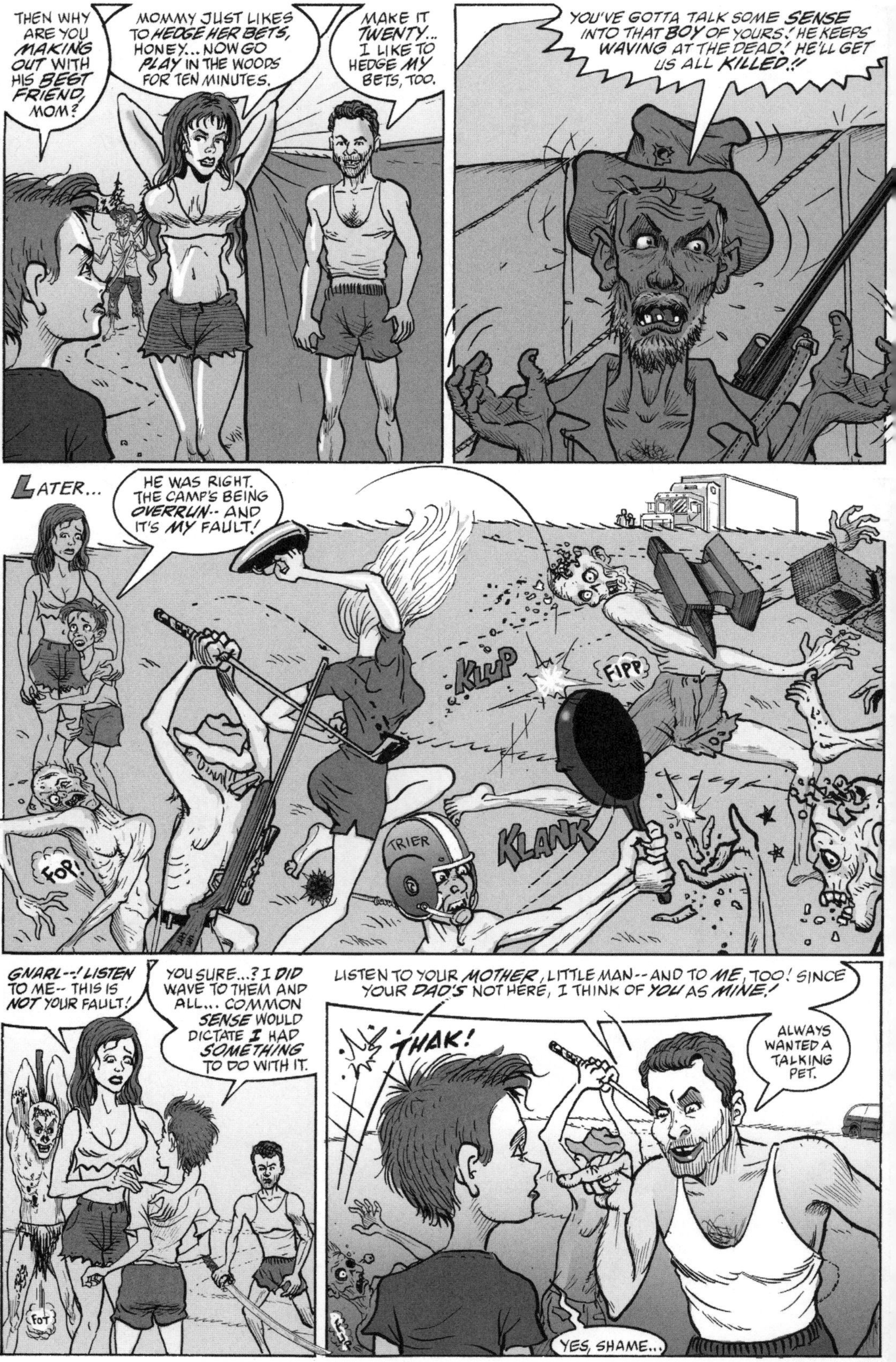
THEN WHY ARE YOU MAKING OUT WITH HIS BEST FRIEND, MOM?
MOMMY JUST LIKES TO HEDGE HER BETS, HONEY... NOW GO PLAY IN THE WOODS FOR TEN MINUTES.
MAKE IT TWENTY... I LIKE TO HEDGE MY BETS, TOO.
YOU'VE GOTTA TALK SOME SENSE INTO THAT BOY OF YOURS! HE KEEPS WAVING AT THE DEAD! HE'LL GET US ALL KILLED!!
LATER...
HE WAS RIGHT. THE CAMP'S BEING OVERRUN-- AND IT'S MY FAULT!
KLUP
FIPP
FOP!
TRIER
KLANK
GNARL--! LISTEN TO ME-- THIS IS NOT YOUR FAULT!
YOU SURE...? I DID WAVE TO THEM AND ALL... COMMON SENSE WOULD DICTATE I HAD SOMETHING TO DO WITH IT.
FOT
LISTEN TO YOUR MOTHER, LITTLE MAN-- AND TO ME, TOO! SINCE YOUR DAD'S NOT HERE, I THINK OF YOU AS MINE!
THAK!
ALWAYS WANTED A TALKING PET.
YES, SHAME...

NOW, WHAT'D WE SAY ABOUT YOU *PLAYING* IN THE WOODS?

THAT I SHOULD GO DO THAT?

--BUT YOU'RE STILL *HERE*, AREN'T YOU?

"AFTER A STOP AT MY HOUSE FOR SOME *CLOTHES* THAT DIDN'T LEAVE MY BUTT HANGING IN THE *WIND*, I SEARCHED FOR MY *FAMILY*."

YOU SEEN A *LITTLE GUY*-- ABOUT YO HIGH?

FORP

"BUT IT PROVED MORE *DIFFICULT* THAN I HAD IMAGINED."

YOU SEEN A SEXY *WOMAN* WITH BLACK HAIR WHO'S ALWAYS LOOKING *DREAMILY* AT MY BEST FRIEND?

FRRRRP-P-P

" *WHATEVER* HAPPENED, I HAD TO HOLD ONTO MY *HUMANITY*. I WOULD *NOT* BECOME ONE OF THOSE MEN WHO *REFUSE TO ASK DIRECTIONS*."

EXCUSE ME, BUT--

THEY'RE COMING FOR YOU, *BARBARA*--! THERE'S ONE OF THEM *NOW*!

FIP FIP

POOF

GLUGG R.I.P.

I HEARD...THERE..!! *OW!!* WAS A CAMP OF SURVIVORS UP ON THAT-- *OW!* HILL!

BI: TE

KRUNCH

FEEEWWWWW

THANK YOU KINDLY. SAY, BUDDY--DOES THAT REALLY TASTE LIKE *CHICKEN?*

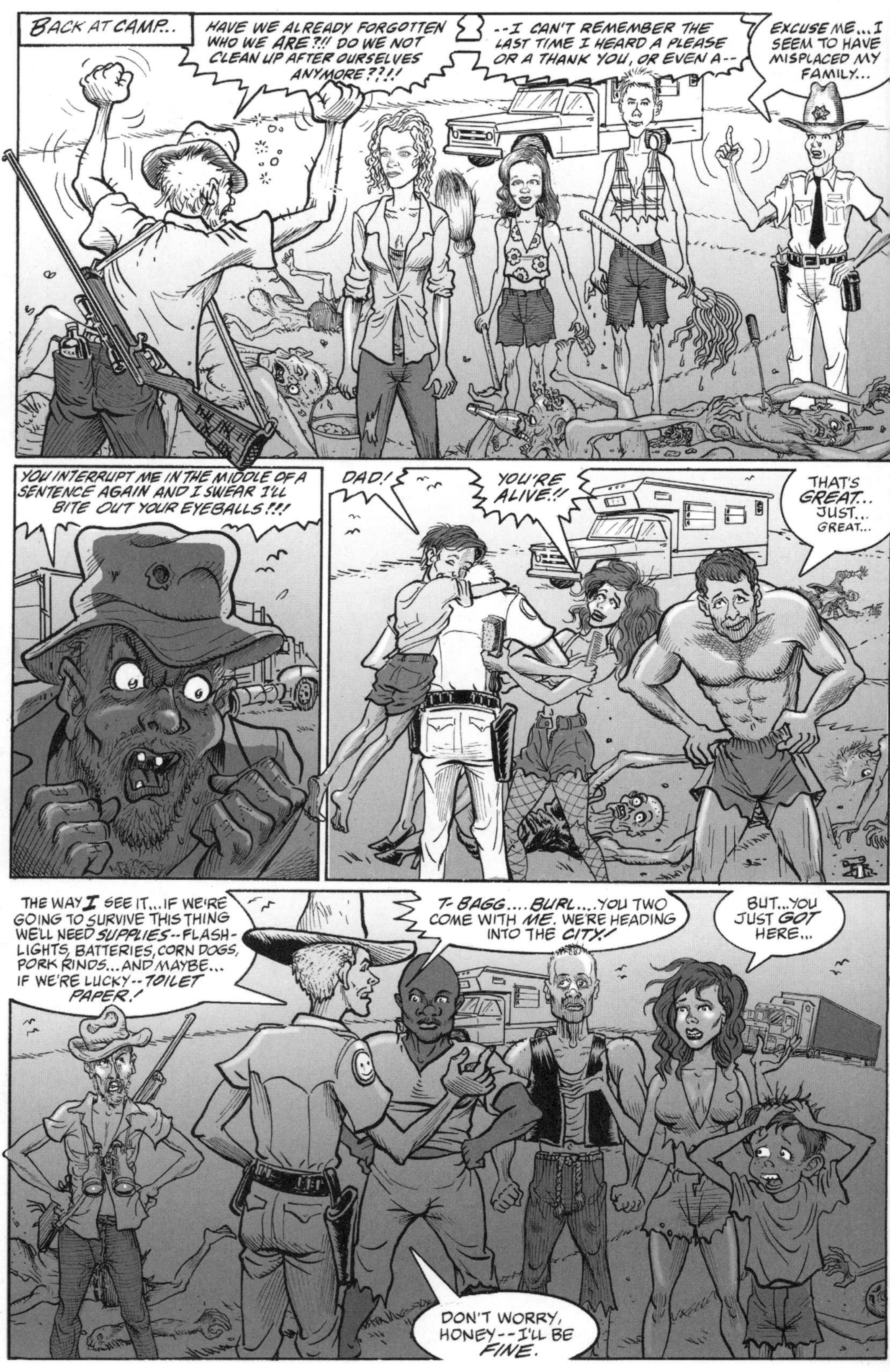
BACK AT CAMP...
HAVE WE ALREADY FORGOTTEN WHO WE ARE?!! DO WE NOT CLEAN UP AFTER OURSELVES ANYMORE??!!
--I CAN'T REMEMBER THE LAST TIME I HEARD A PLEASE OR A THANK YOU, OR EVEN A--
EXCUSE ME...I SEEM TO HAVE MISPLACED MY FAMILY...
YOU INTERRUPT ME IN THE MIDDLE OF A SENTENCE AGAIN AND I SWEAR I'LL BITE OUT YOUR EYEBALLS!!!
DAD!
YOU'RE ALIVE!!
THAT'S GREAT... JUST... GREAT...
THE WAY I SEE IT...IF WE'RE GOING TO SURVIVE THIS THING WE'LL NEED SUPPLIES--FLASHLIGHTS, BATTERIES, CORN DOGS, PORK RINDS...AND MAYBE... IF WE'RE LUCKY--TOILET PAPER!
T-BAGG....BURL....YOU TWO COME WITH ME. WE'RE HEADING INTO THE CITY!
BUT...YOU JUST GOT HERE...
DON'T WORRY, HONEY--I'LL BE FINE.

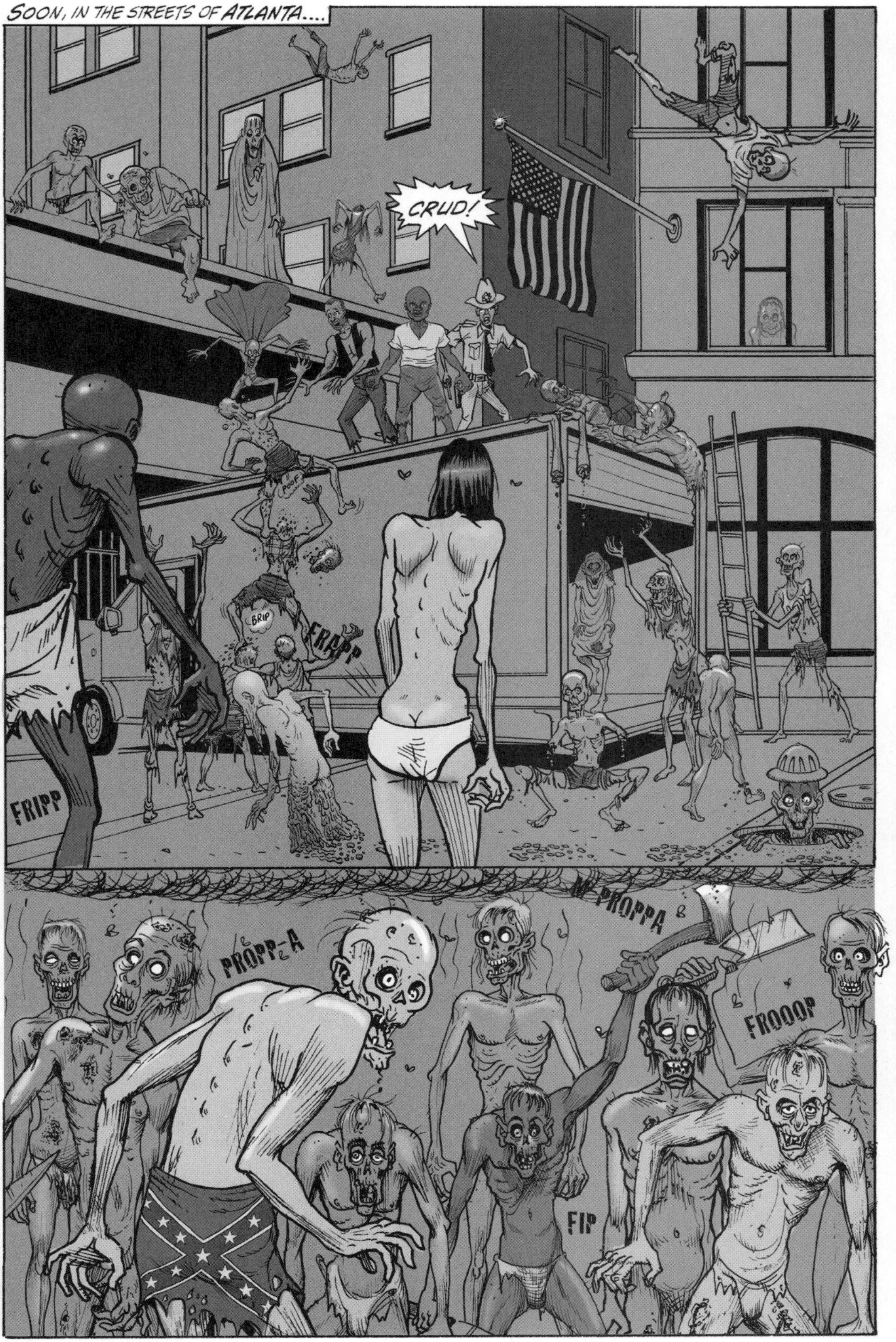
SOON, IN THE STREETS OF ATLANTA....
CRUD!
POOF
BRIP
FRAPP
FRIPP
PROPPA
PROPP-A
FROOOP
FIP

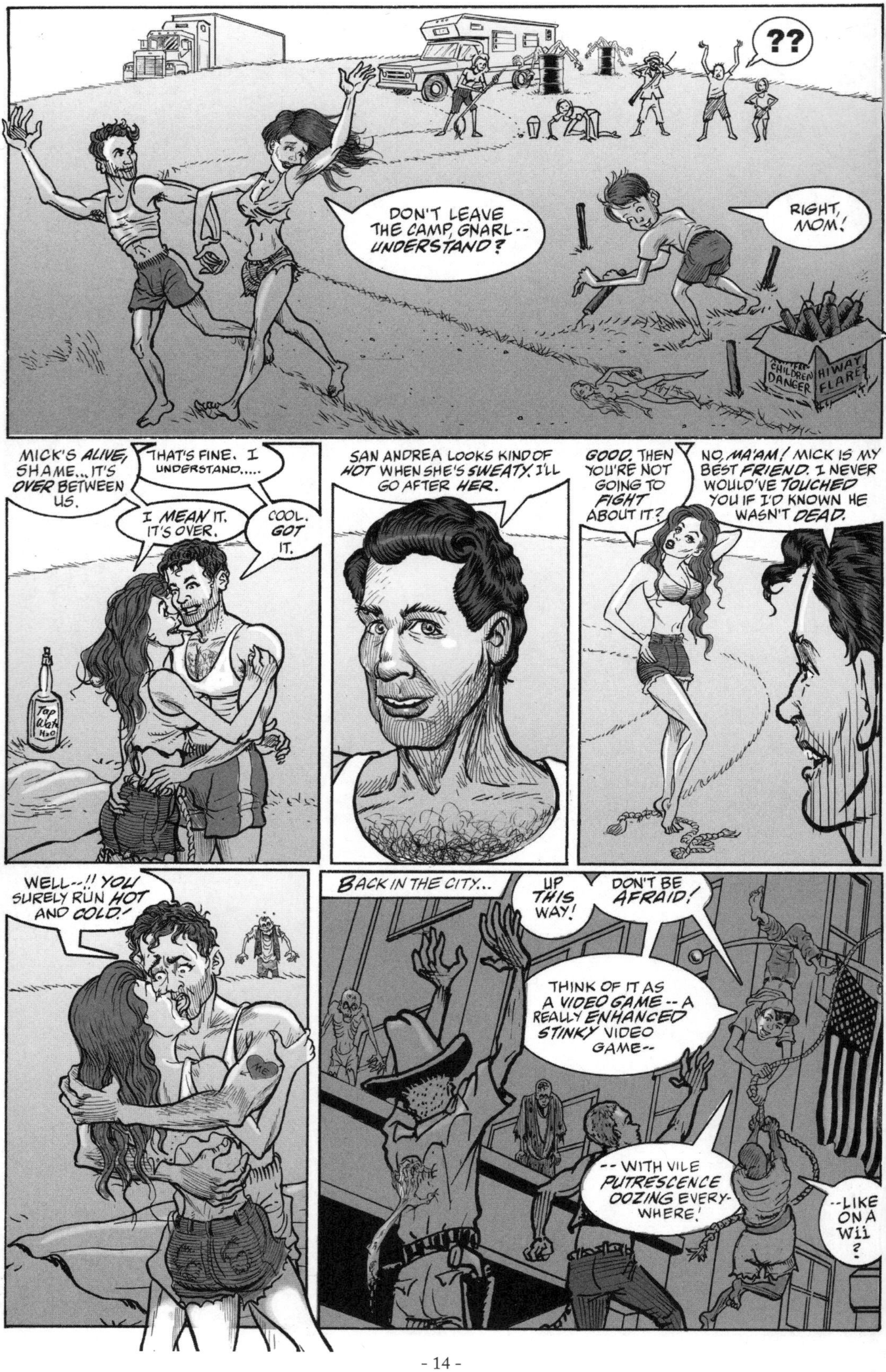
??
DON'T LEAVE THE CAMP, GNARL-- UNDERSTAND?
RIGHT, MOM!
CHILDREN DANGER
HIWAY FLARES
MICK'S ALIVE, SHAME... IT'S OVER BETWEEN US.
THAT'S FINE. I UNDERSTAND.....
I MEAN IT. IT'S OVER.
COOL. GOT IT.
Tap Water H2O
SAN ANDREA LOOKS KIND OF HOT WHEN SHE'S SWEATY. I'LL GO AFTER HER.
GOOD. THEN YOU'RE NOT GOING TO FIGHT ABOUT IT?
NO, MA'AM! MICK IS MY BEST FRIEND. I NEVER WOULD'VE TOUCHED YOU IF I'D KNOWN HE WASN'T DEAD.
WELL--!! YOU SURELY RUN HOT AND COLD!
ME
BACK IN THE CITY...
UP THIS WAY!
DON'T BE AFRAID!
THINK OF IT AS A VIDEO GAME -- A REALLY ENHANCED STINKY VIDEO GAME--
--WITH VILE PUTRESCENCE OOZING EVERY-WHERE!
--LIKE ON A Wii?

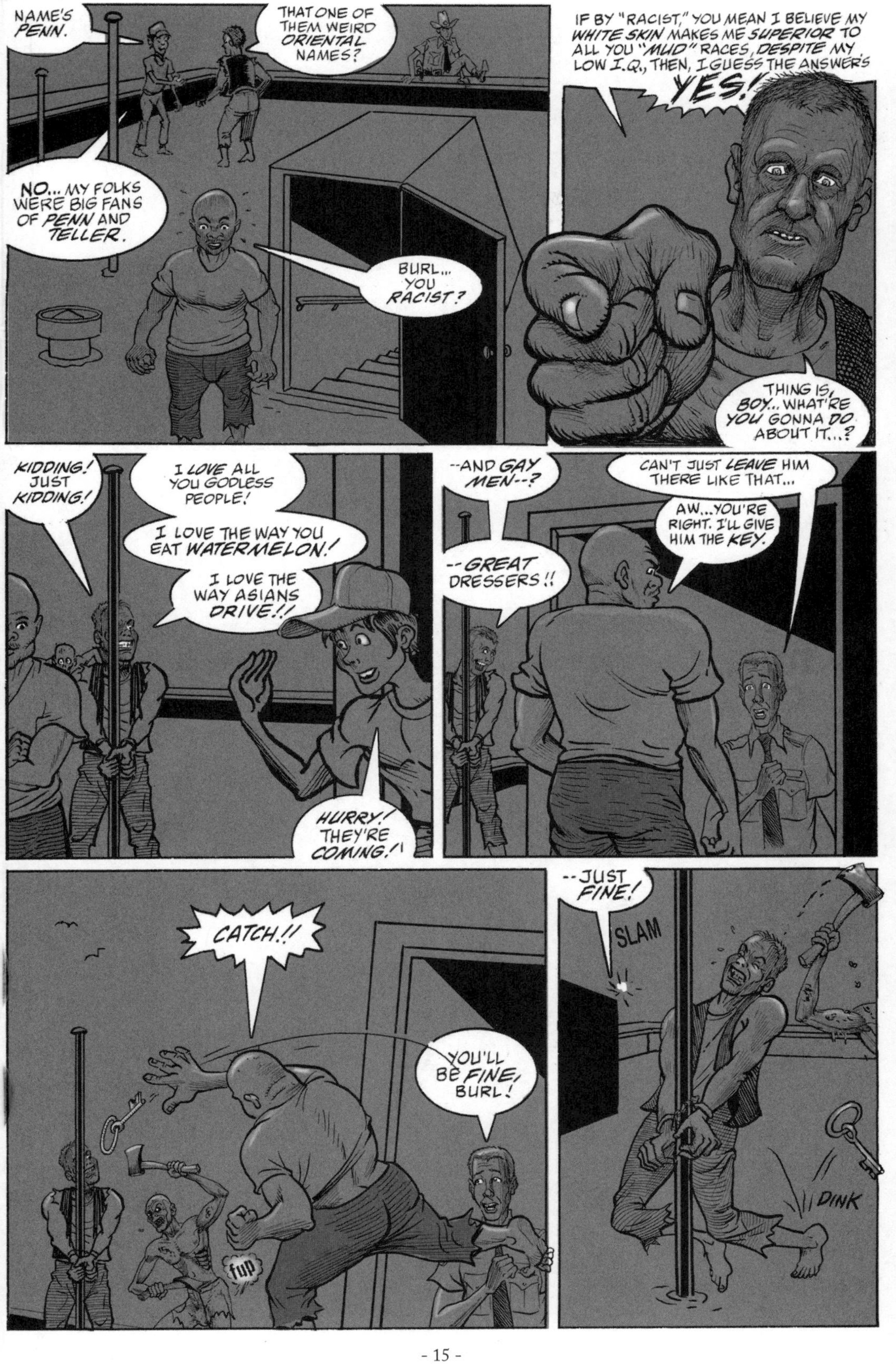
NAME'S PENN.
THAT ONE OF THEM WEIRD ORIENTAL NAMES?
NO... MY FOLKS WERE BIG FANS OF PENN AND TELLER.
BURL... YOU RACIST?
IF BY "RACIST," YOU MEAN I BELIEVE MY WHITE SKIN MAKES ME SUPERIOR TO ALL YOU "MUD" RACES, DESPITE MY LOW I.Q., THEN, I GUESS THE ANSWER'S YES!
THING IS, BOY... WHAT'RE YOU GONNA DO ABOUT IT...?
KIDDING! JUST KIDDING!
I LOVE ALL YOU GODLESS PEOPLE!
I LOVE THE WAY YOU EAT WATERMELON!
I LOVE THE WAY ASIANS DRIVE!!
HURRY! THEY'RE COMING!!
--AND GAY MEN--?
--GREAT DRESSERS!!
CAN'T JUST LEAVE HIM THERE LIKE THAT...
AW...YOU'RE RIGHT. I'LL GIVE HIM THE KEY.
CATCH!!
YOU'LL BE FINE, BURL!
fup
--JUST FINE!
SLAM
DINK

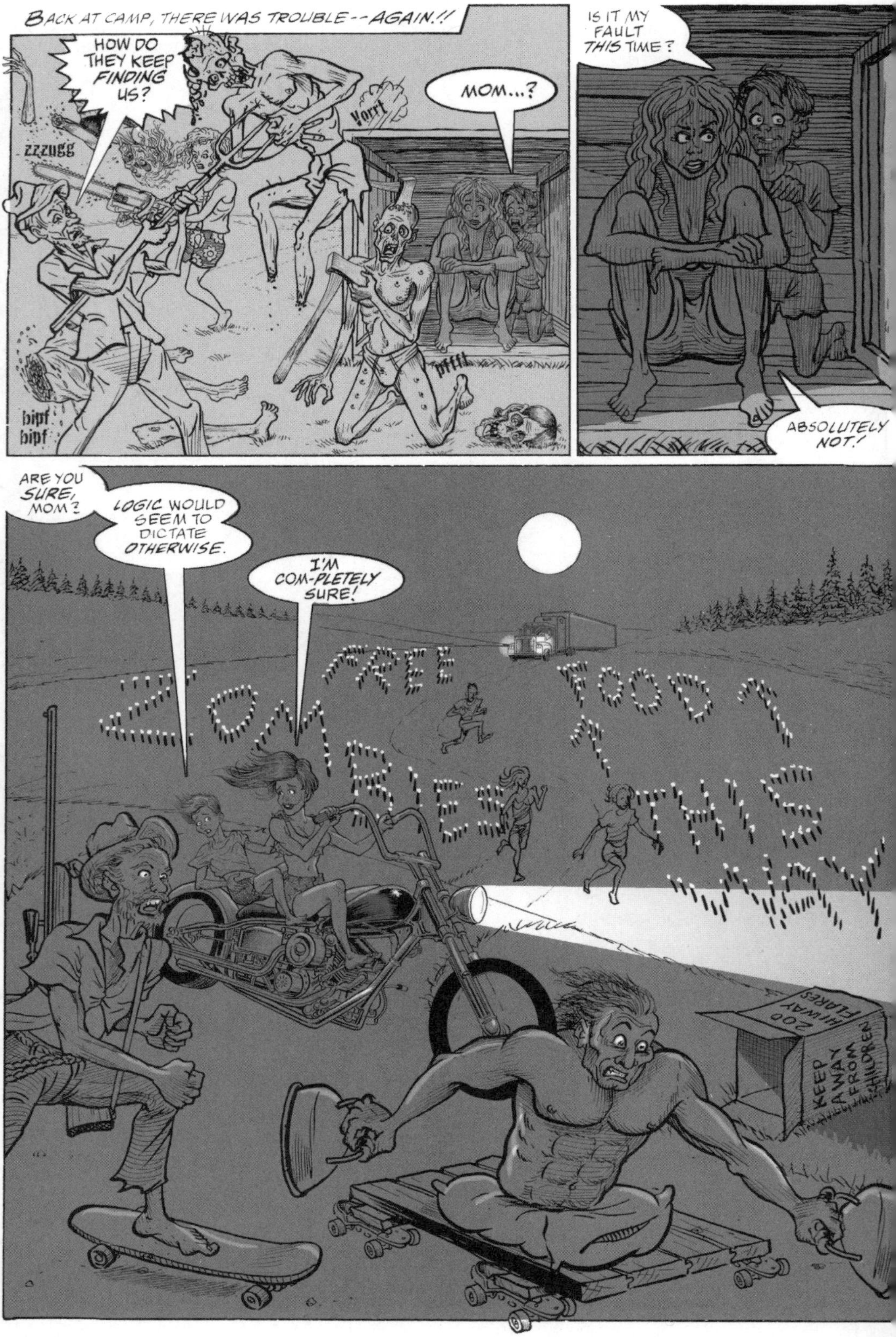
BACK AT CAMP, THERE WAS TROUBLE--AGAIN!!
HOW DO THEY KEEP FINDING US?
zzzugg
vorrt
MOM...?
pffft
bipf bipf
IS IT MY FAULT THIS TIME?
ABSOLUTELY NOT!
ARE YOU SURE, MOM?
LOGIC WOULD SEEM TO DICTATE OTHERWISE.
I'M COM-PLETELY SURE!
ZOMBIES
FREE FOOD
THIS WAY
200 HIWAY FLARES
KEEP AWAY FROM CHILDREN

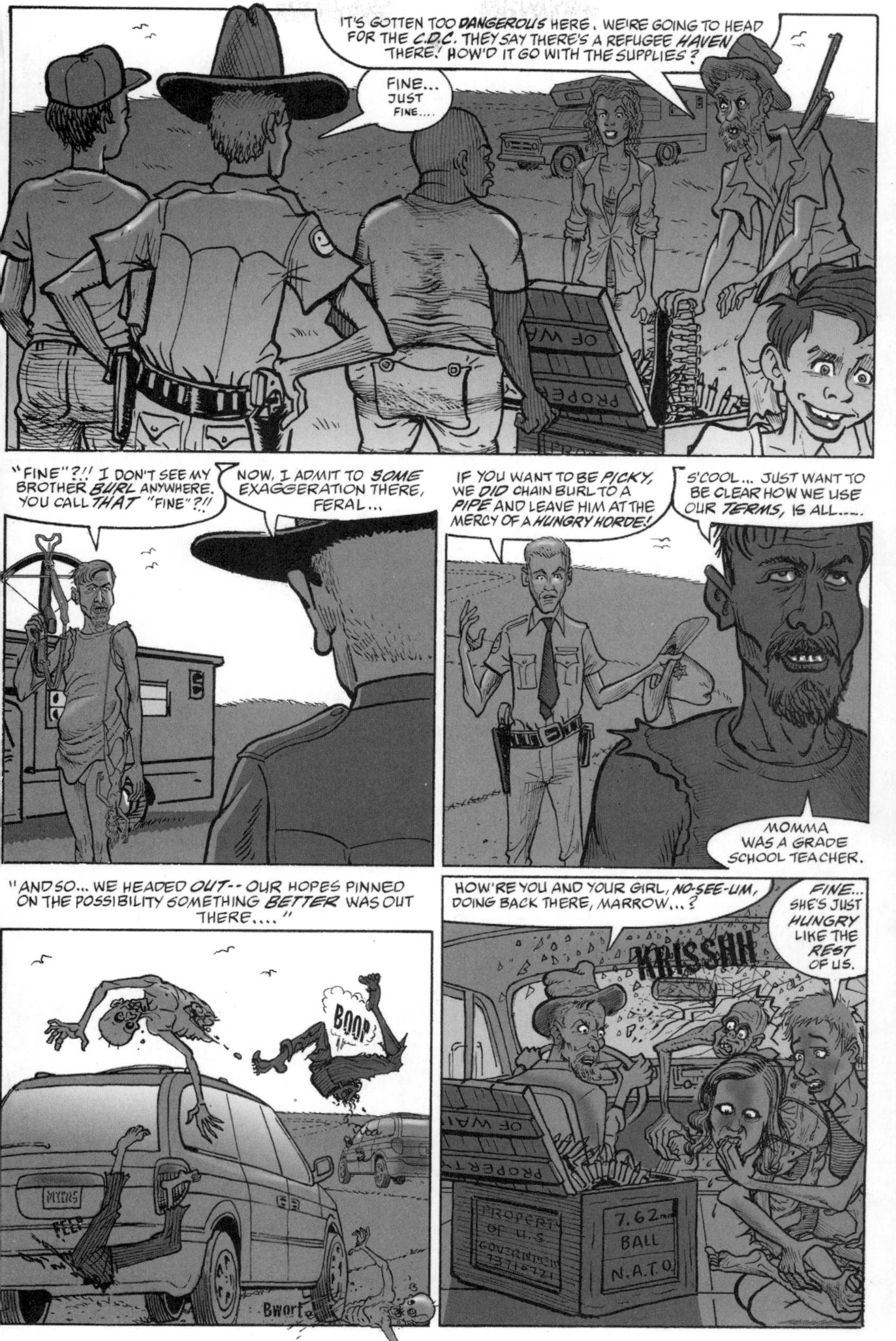
IT'S GOTTEN TOO DANGEROUS HERE. WE'RE GOING TO HEAD FOR THE C.D.C. THEY SAY THERE'S A REFUGEE HAVEN THERE! HOW'D IT GO WITH THE SUPPLIES?
FINE... JUST FINE....
"FINE"?!! I DON'T SEE MY BROTHER BURL ANYWHERE. YOU CALL THAT "FINE"?!!
NOW, I ADMIT TO SOME EXAGGERATION THERE, FERAL...
IF YOU WANT TO BE PICKY, WE DID CHAIN BURL TO A PIPE AND LEAVE HIM AT THE MERCY OF A HUNGRY HORDE!
S'COOL... JUST WANT TO BE CLEAR HOW WE USE OUR TERMS, IS ALL....
MOMMA WAS A GRADE SCHOOL TEACHER.
"AND SO... WE HEADED OUT-- OUR HOPES PINNED ON THE POSSIBILITY SOMETHING BETTER WAS OUT THERE...."
BOOP
Bwort
HOW'RE YOU AND YOUR GIRL, NO-SEE-UM, DOING BACK THERE, MARROW...?
FINE... SHE'S JUST HUNGRY LIKE THE REST OF US.
KRISSHH
PROPERTY OF U.S. GOVERNMENT
7.62mm BALL N.A.T.O.

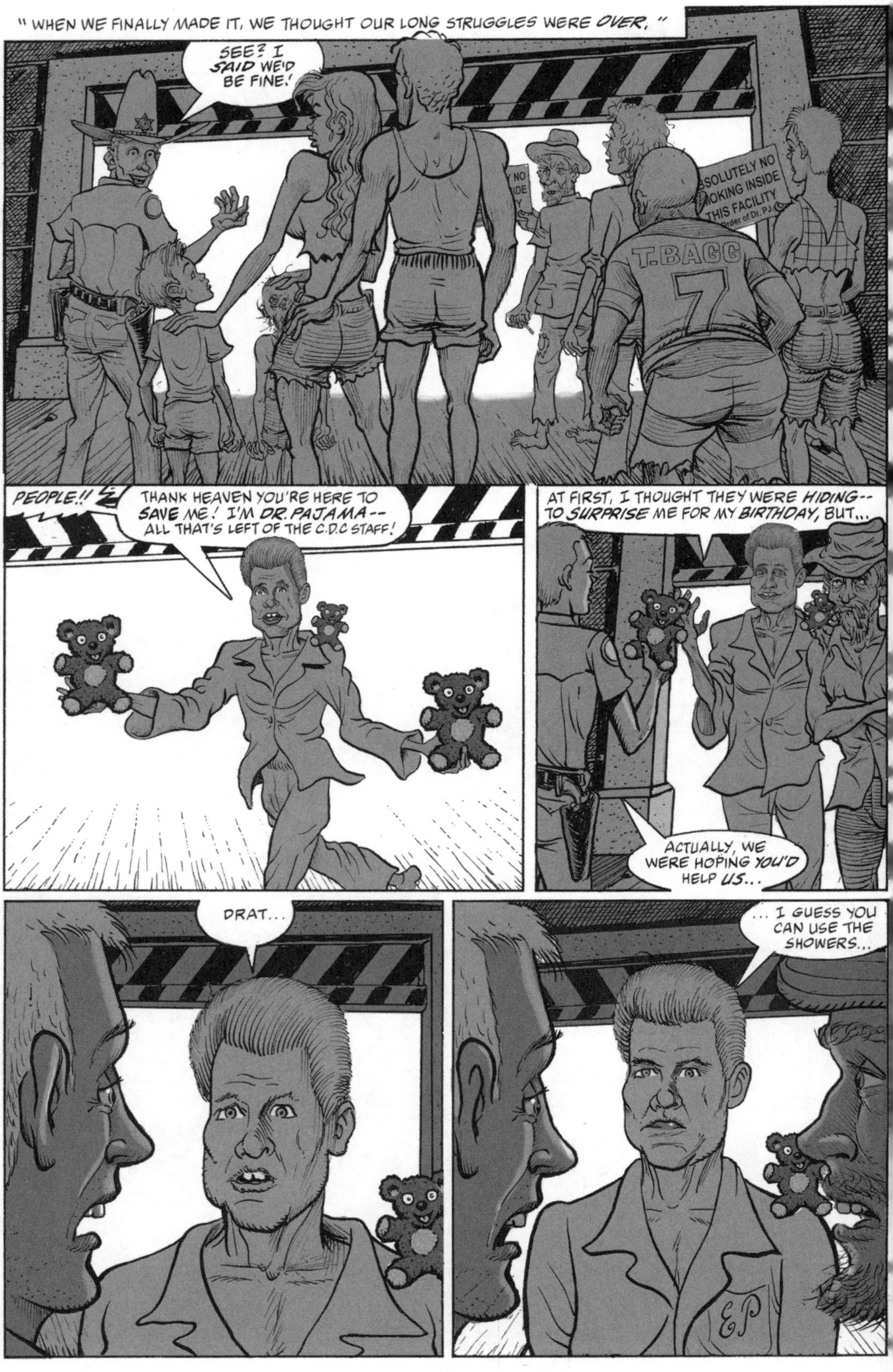
" WHEN WE FINALLY MADE IT, WE THOUGHT OUR LONG STRUGGLES WERE OVER. "
SEE? I SAID WE'D BE FINE!
SOLUTELY NO
OKING INSIDE
THIS FACILITY
Order of Dr. PJ
T.BAGG
7
PEOPLE!!
THANK HEAVEN YOU'RE HERE TO SAVE ME! I'M DR. PAJAMA-- ALL THAT'S LEFT OF THE C.D.C STAFF!
AT FIRST, I THOUGHT THEY WERE HIDING-- TO SURPRISE ME FOR MY BIRTHDAY, BUT...
ACTUALLY, WE WERE HOPING YOU'D HELP US...
DRAT...
... I GUESS YOU CAN USE THE SHOWERS...

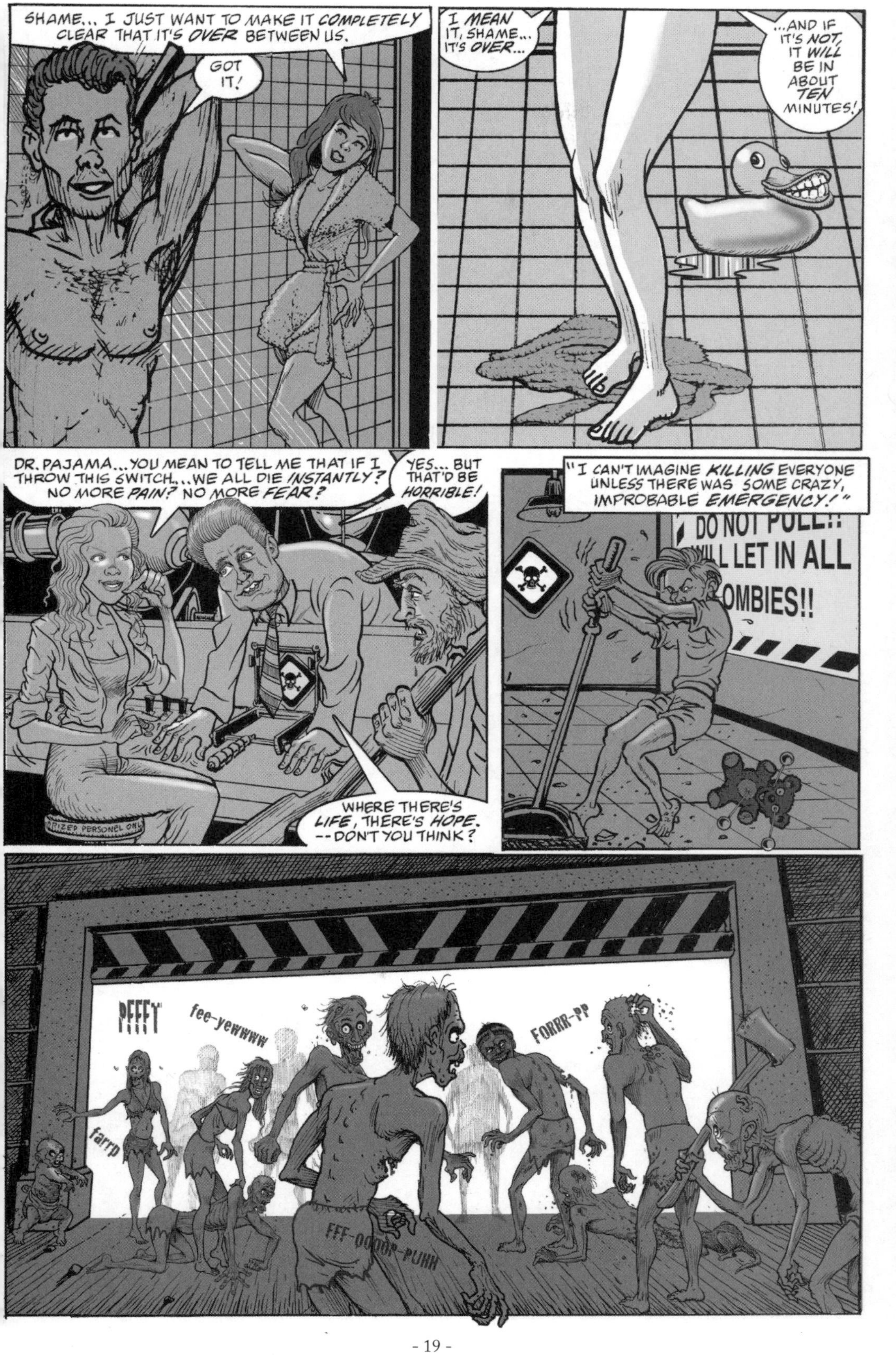
SHAME... I JUST WANT TO MAKE IT COMPLETELY CLEAR THAT IT'S OVER BETWEEN US.
GOT IT!
I MEAN IT, SHAME... IT'S OVER...
...AND IF IT'S NOT, IT WILL BE IN ABOUT TEN MINUTES!
DR. PAJAMA... YOU MEAN TO TELL ME THAT IF I THROW THIS SWITCH... WE ALL DIE INSTANTLY? NO MORE PAIN? NO MORE FEAR?
YES... BUT THAT'D BE HORRIBLE!
WHERE THERE'S LIFE, THERE'S HOPE. --DON'T YOU THINK?
"I CAN'T IMAGINE KILLING EVERYONE UNLESS THERE WAS SOME CRAZY, IMPROBABLE EMERGENCY!"
DO NOT PULL!!
ILL LET IN ALL
OMBIES!!
PFFFT
fee-yewwww
farrp
FORRR-PP
FFF-OOOOP-PUHH

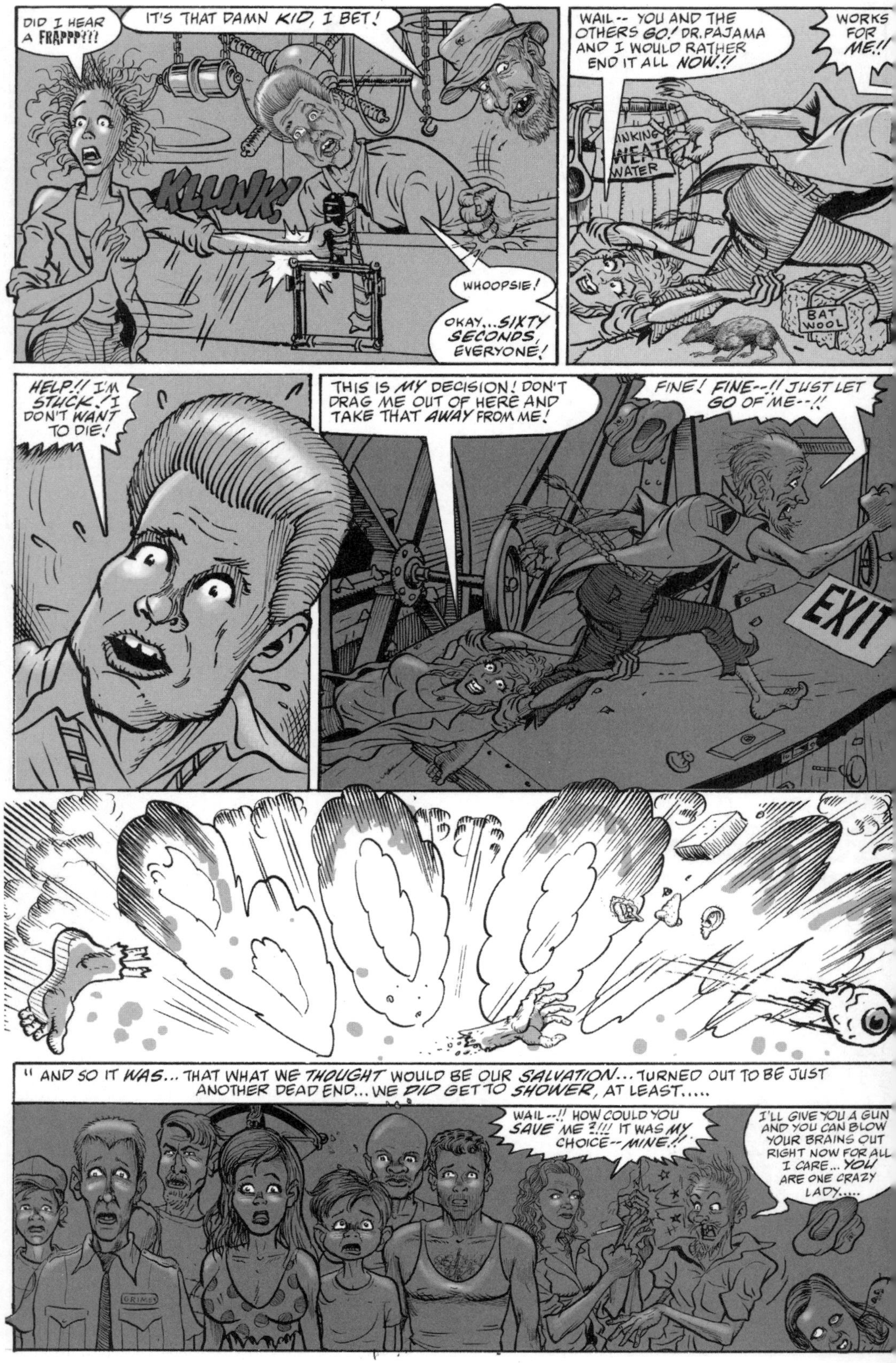
DID I HEAR A FRAPPP???
IT'S THAT DAMN KID, I BET!
KLUNK!
WHOOPSIE!
OKAY... SIXTY SECONDS, EVERYONE!
WAIL -- YOU AND THE OTHERS GO! DR. PAJAMA AND I WOULD RATHER END IT ALL NOW!!
WORKS FOR ME!!
BAT WOOL
HELP!! I'M STUCK! I DON'T WANT TO DIE!
THIS IS MY DECISION! DON'T DRAG ME OUT OF HERE AND TAKE THAT AWAY FROM ME!
FINE! FINE--!! JUST LET GO OF ME--!!
EXIT
" AND SO IT WAS... THAT WHAT WE THOUGHT WOULD BE OUR SALVATION... TURNED OUT TO BE JUST ANOTHER DEAD END... WE DID GET TO SHOWER, AT LEAST.....
WAIL--!! HOW COULD YOU SAVE ME ?!!! IT WAS MY CHOICE-- MINE!!
I'LL GIVE YOU A GUN AND YOU CAN BLOW YOUR BRAINS OUT RIGHT NOW FOR ALL I CARE... YOU ARE ONE CRAZY LADY.....
GRIMES

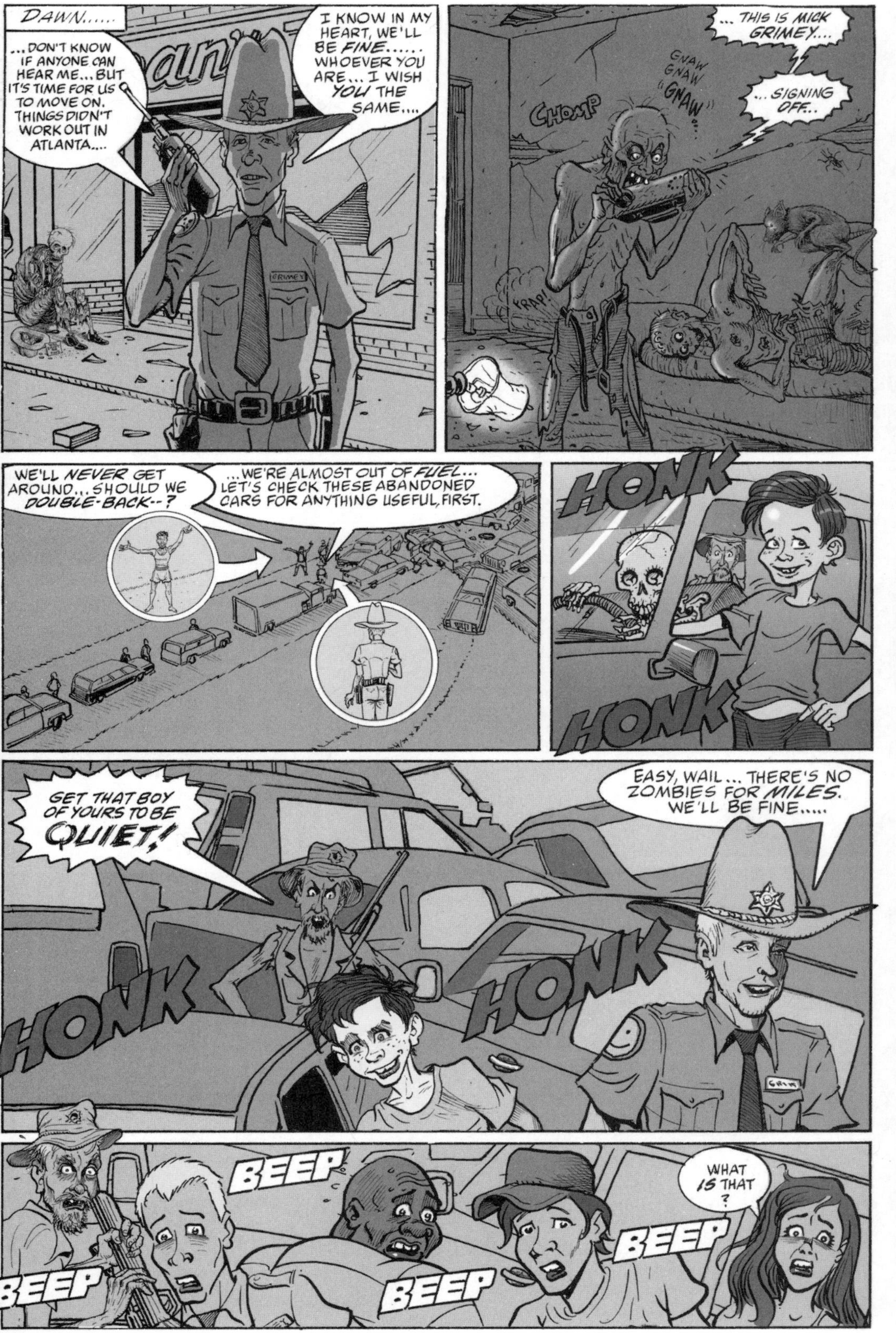

DAWN......
...DON'T KNOW IF ANYONE CAN HEAR ME... BUT IT'S TIME FOR US TO MOVE ON. THINGS DIDN'T WORK OUT IN ATLANTA....
I KNOW IN MY HEART, WE'LL BE FINE...... WHOEVER YOU ARE... I WISH YOU THE SAME....
GRIMEY
... THIS IS MICK GRIMEY....
GNAW GNAW GNAW
CHOMP
... SIGNING OFF..
FRAP!
WE'LL NEVER GET AROUND... SHOULD WE DOUBLE-BACK--?
...WE'RE ALMOST OUT OF FUEL... LET'S CHECK THESE ABANDONED CARS FOR ANYTHING USEFUL, FIRST.
HONK
HONK
GET THAT BOY OF YOURS TO BE QUIET!
EASY, WAIL... THERE'S NO ZOMBIES FOR MILES. WE'LL BE FINE.....
HONK
HONK
BEEP
WHAT IS THAT ?
BEEP
BEEP
BEEP

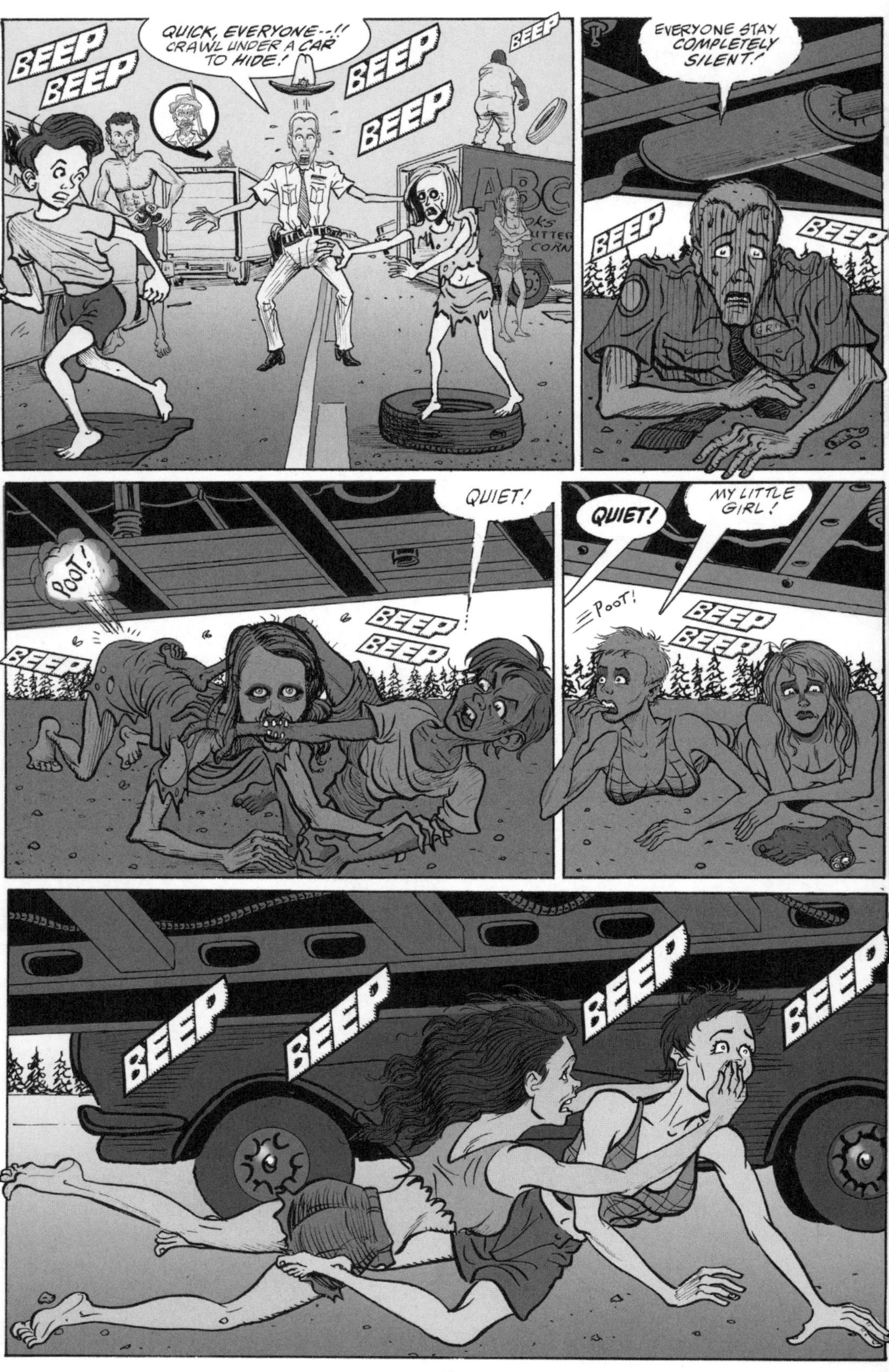
BEEP
BEEP
QUICK, EVERYONE--!! CRAWL UNDER A CAR TO HIDE!
BEEP
BEEP
BEEP
BEEP
EVERYONE STAY COMPLETELY SILENT!
BEEP
BEEP
POOT!
BEEP
BEEP
BEEP
QUIET!
QUIET!
MY LITTLE GIRL!
POOT!
BEEP
BEEP
BEEP
BEEP
BEEP
BEEP

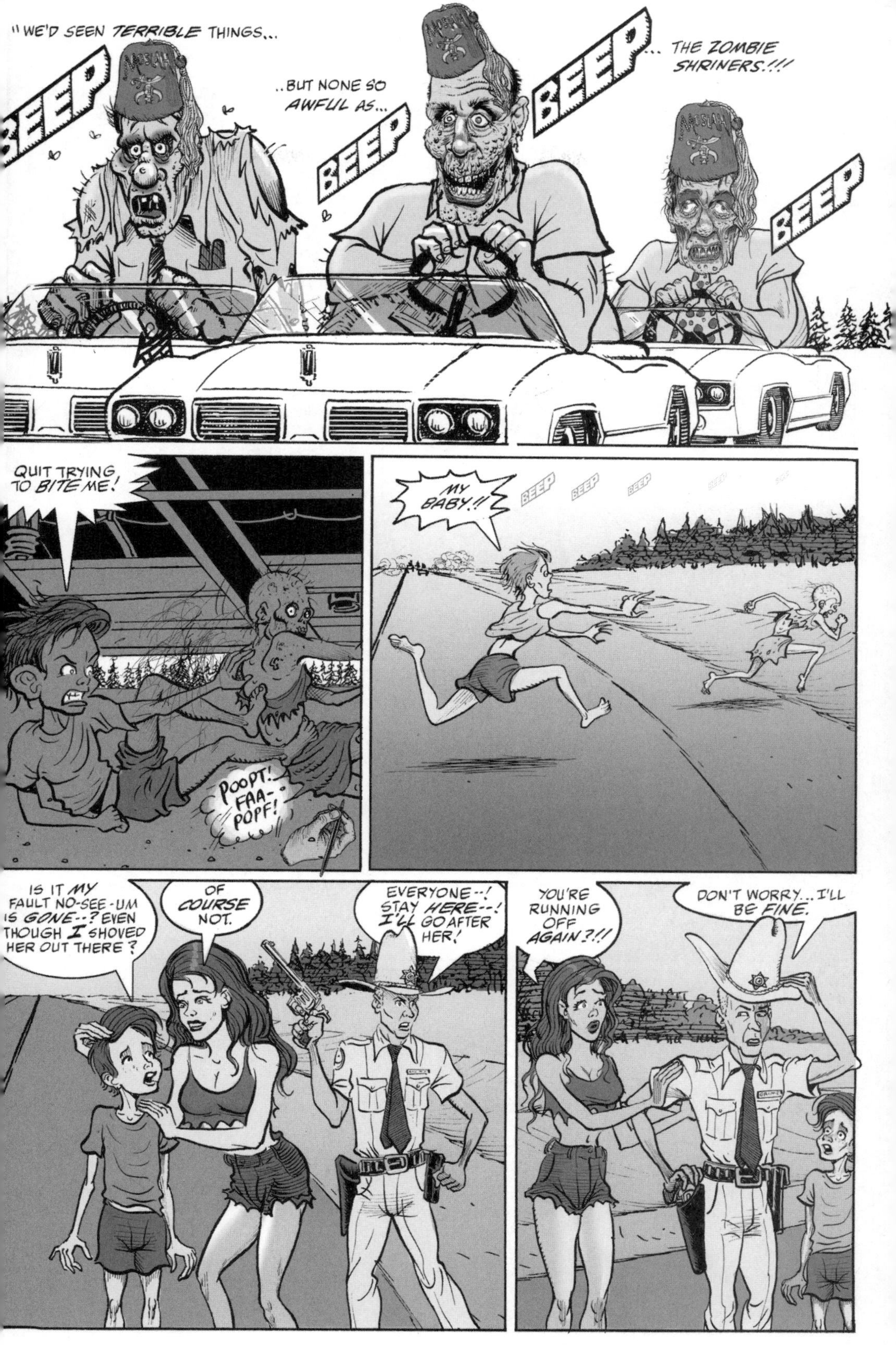
"WE'D SEEN TERRIBLE THINGS...
BEEP
..BUT NONE SO AWFUL AS...
BEEP
BEEP
... THE ZOMBIE SHRINERS!!!
BEEP
QUIT TRYING TO BITE ME!
POOPT! FAA-POPF!
MY BABY!!
BEEP
BEEP
BEEP
IS IT MY FAULT NO-SEE-UM IS GONE--? EVEN THOUGH I SHOVED HER OUT THERE?
OF COURSE NOT.
EVERYONE--! STAY HERE--! I'LL GO AFTER HER!
YOU'RE RUNNING OFF AGAIN?!!
DON'T WORRY... I'LL BE FINE.

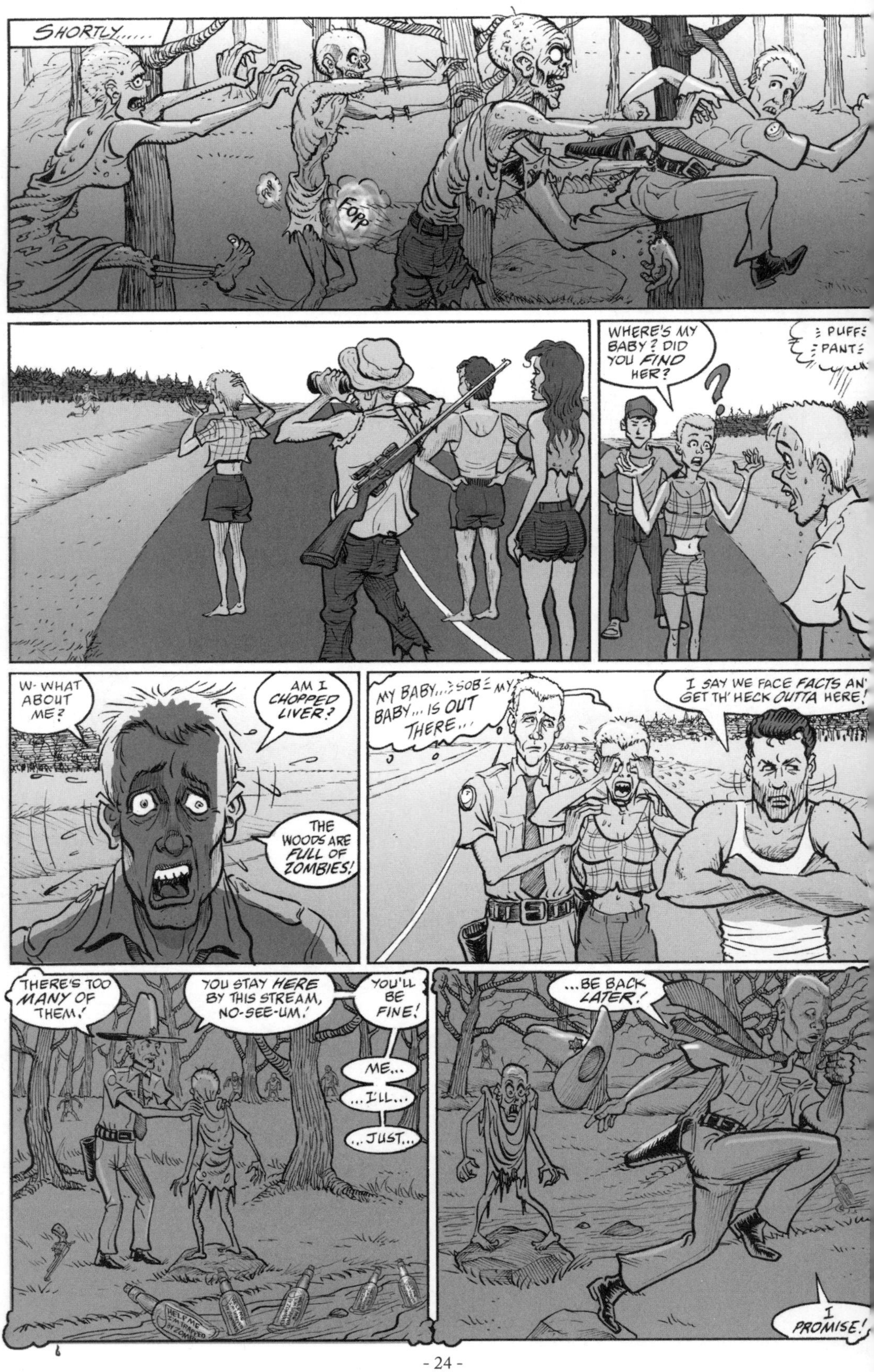
SHORTLY.....
FOPP
WHERE'S MY BABY? DID YOU FIND HER?
PUFF PANT
W- WHAT ABOUT ME?
AM I CHOPPED LIVER?
THE WOODS ARE FULL OF ZOMBIES!
MY BABY... SOB MY BABY... IS OUT THERE...
I SAY WE FACE FACTS AN' GET TH' HECK OUTTA HERE!
THERE'S TOO MANY OF THEM!
YOU STAY HERE BY THIS STREAM, NO-SEE-UM!
YOU'LL BE FINE!
ME...
...I'LL...
...JUST...
...BE BACK LATER!
I PROMISE!

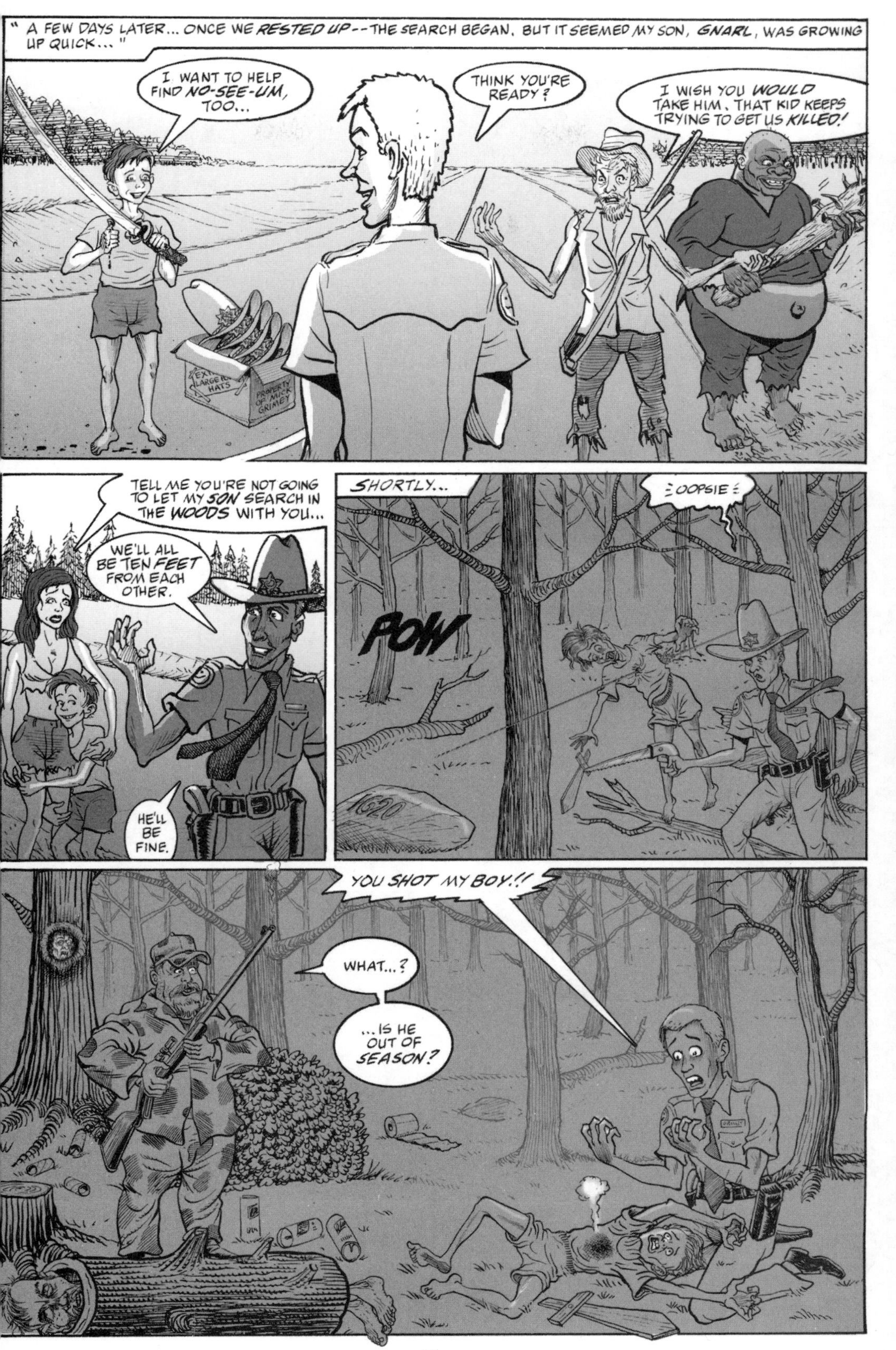

" A FEW DAYS LATER... ONCE WE RESTED UP -- THE SEARCH BEGAN. BUT IT SEEMED MY SON, GNARL, WAS GROWING UP QUICK... "
I WANT TO HELP FIND NO-SEE-UM, TOO...
THINK YOU'RE READY?
I WISH YOU WOULD TAKE HIM. THAT KID KEEPS TRYING TO GET US KILLED!
PROPERTY OF MICK GRIMEY
TELL ME YOU'RE NOT GOING TO LET MY SON SEARCH IN THE WOODS WITH YOU...
WE'LL ALL BE TEN FEET FROM EACH OTHER.
HE'LL BE FINE.
SHORTLY...
OOPSIE
POW
YOU SHOT MY BOY!!
WHAT...?
...IS HE OUT OF SEASON?

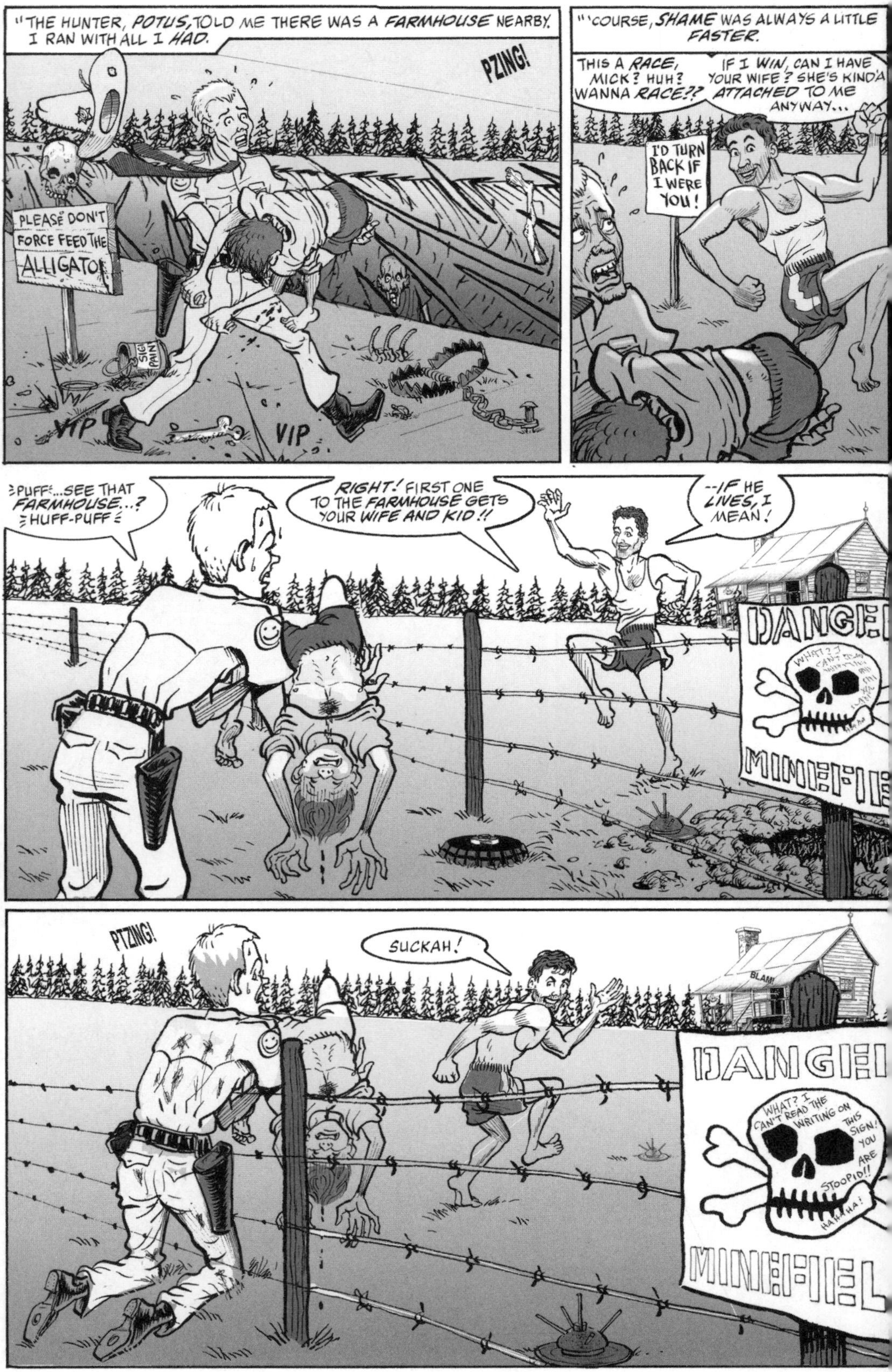
"THE HUNTER, POTUS, TOLD ME THERE WAS A FARMHOUSE NEARBY. I RAN WITH ALL I HAD.
PZING!
PLEASE DON'T FORCE FEED THE ALLIGATO
VIP
VIP
"'COURSE, SHAME WAS ALWAYS A LITTLE FASTER.
THIS A RACE, MICK? HUH? WANNA RACE??
IF I WIN, CAN I HAVE YOUR WIFE? SHE'S KINDA ATTACHED TO ME ANYWAY...
I'D TURN BACK IF I WERE YOU!
PUFF...SEE THAT FARMHOUSE...? HUFF-PUFF
RIGHT! FIRST ONE TO THE FARMHOUSE GETS YOUR WIFE AND KID!!
--IF HE LIVES, I MEAN!
PTZING!
SUCKAH!
BLAM!
DANGE
WHAT? I CAN'T READ THE WRITING ON THIS SIGN! YOU ARE STOOPID!! HAHAHA!
MINEFIEL

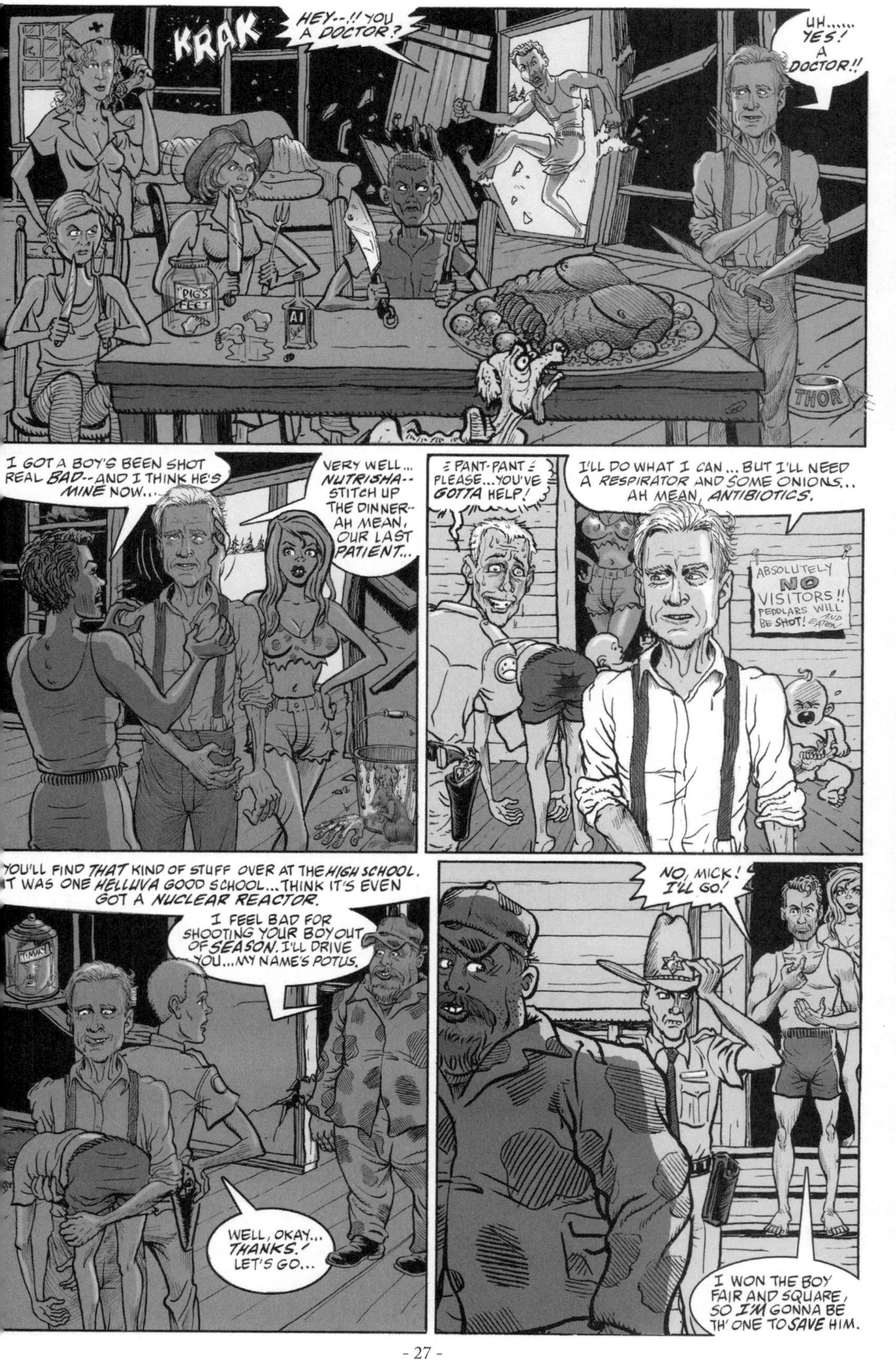

KRAK
HEY--!! YOU A DOCTOR?
UH...... YES! A DOCTOR!!
'PIG'S' FEET
A1
THOR
I GOT A BOY'S BEEN SHOT REAL BAD--AND I THINK HE'S MINE NOW...
VERY WELL... NUTRISHA-- STITCH UP THE DINNER-- AH MEAN, OUR LAST PATIENT...
PANT-PANT PLEASE...YOU'VE GOTTA HELP!
I'LL DO WHAT I CAN... BUT I'LL NEED A RESPIRATOR AND SOME ONIONS... AH MEAN, ANTIBIOTICS.
ABSOLUTELY NO VISITORS!! PEDDLARS WILL BE SHOT! AND EATEN
YOU'LL FIND THAT KIND OF STUFF OVER AT THE HIGH SCHOOL. IT WAS ONE HELLUVA GOOD SCHOOL... THINK IT'S EVEN GOT A NUCLEAR REACTOR.
I FEEL BAD FOR SHOOTING YOUR BOY OUT OF SEASON. I'LL DRIVE YOU...MY NAME'S POTUS.
TIMMY
WELL, OKAY... THANKS! LET'S GO...
NO, MICK! I'LL GO!
I WON THE BOY FAIR AND SQUARE, SO I'M GONNA BE TH' ONE TO SAVE HIM.

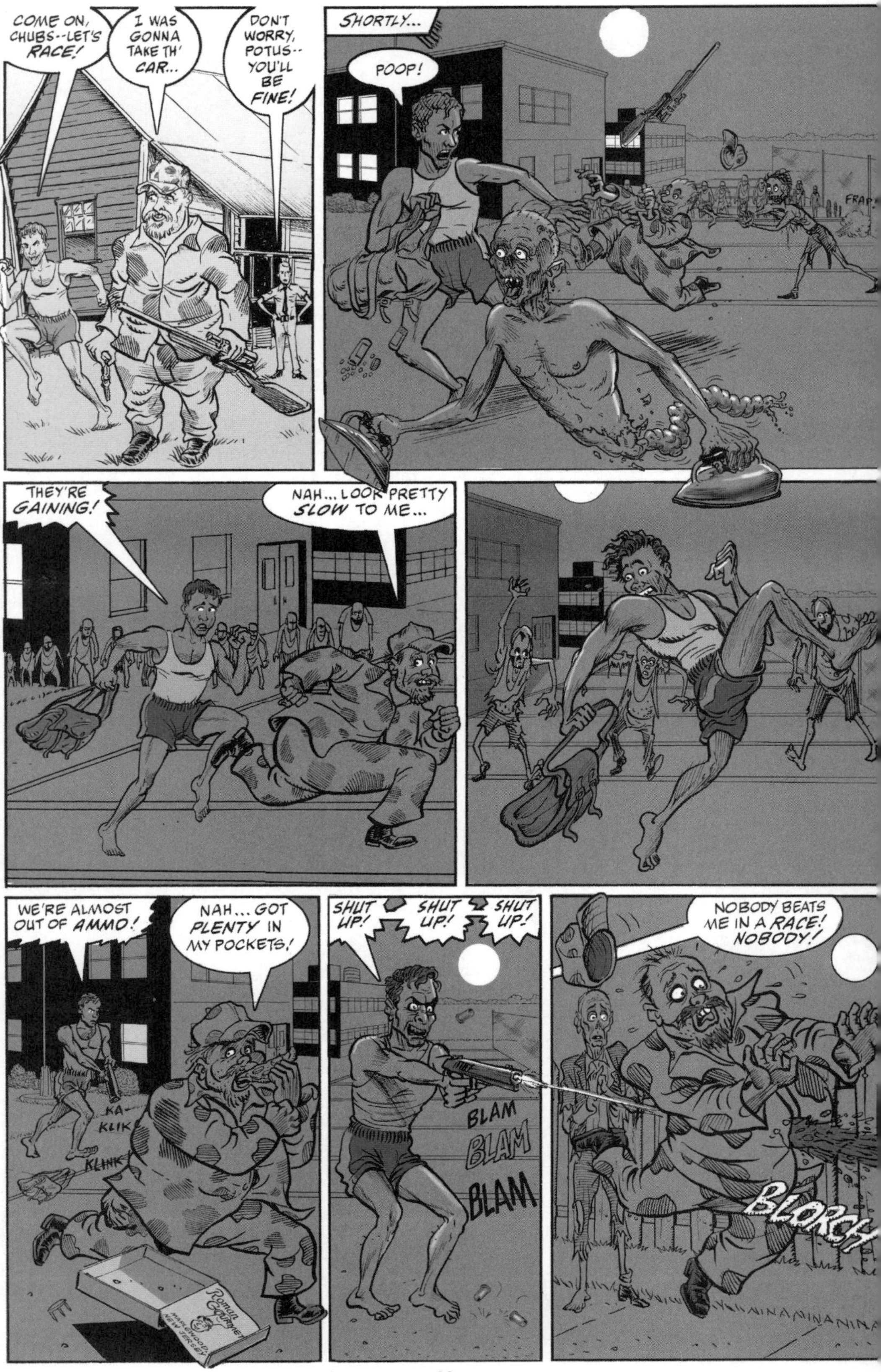
COME ON, CHUBS--LET'S RACE!
I WAS GONNA TAKE TH' CAR...
DON'T WORRY, POTUS-- YOU'LL BE FINE!
SHORTLY...
POOP!
FRAP
THEY'RE GAINING!
NAH... LOOK PRETTY SLOW TO ME...
WE'RE ALMOST OUT OF AMMO!
NAH... GOT PLENTY IN MY POCKETS!
KA-KLIK
KLINK
SHUT UP!
SHUT UP!
SHUT UP!
BLAM
BLAM
BLAM
NOBODY BEATS ME IN A RACE! NOBODY!
BLORCH
NINANINANINANINA

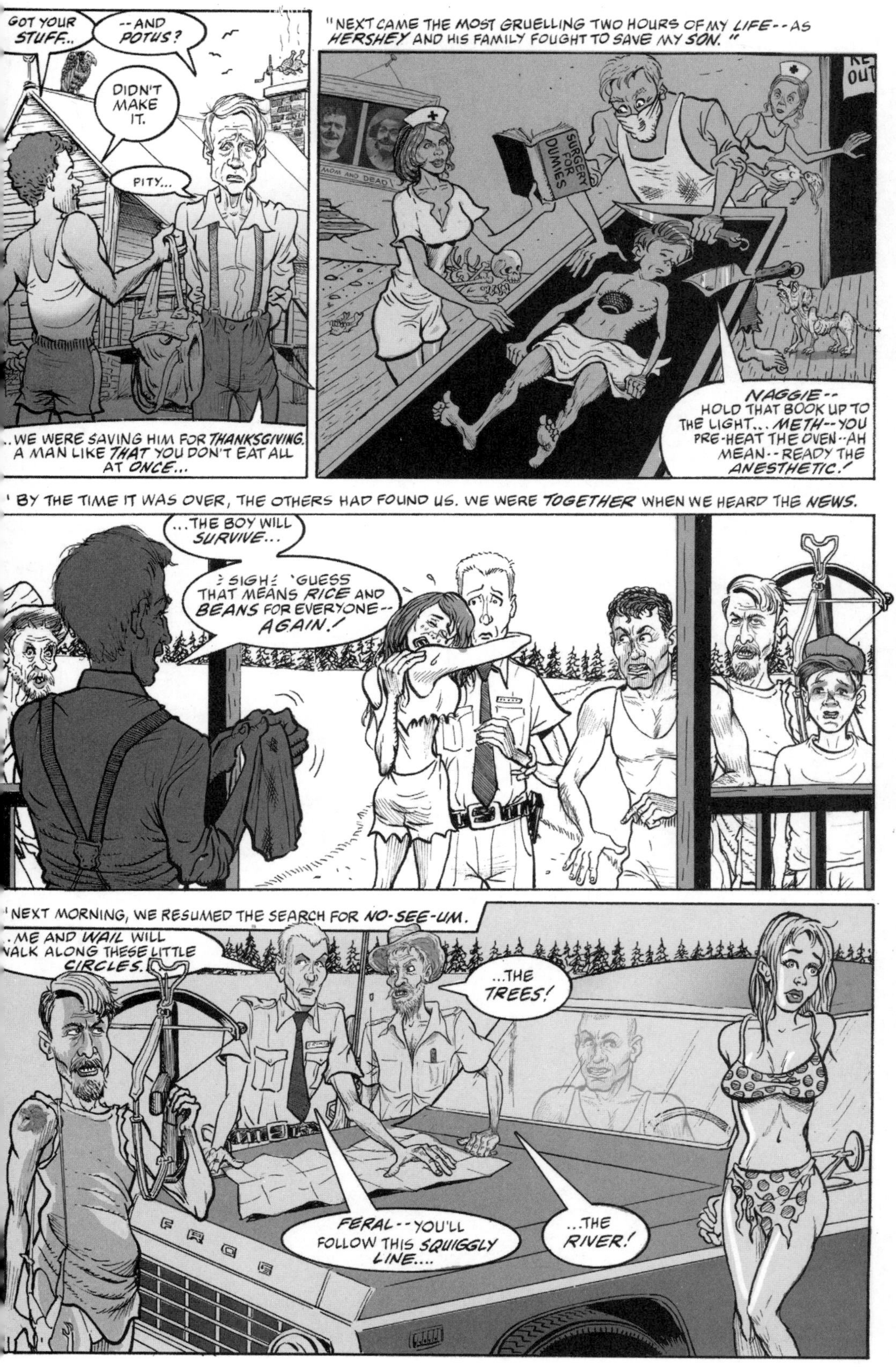
GOT YOUR STUFF...
--AND POTUS?
DIDN'T MAKE IT.
PITY...
..WE WERE SAVING HIM FOR THANKSGIVING. A MAN LIKE THAT YOU DON'T EAT ALL AT ONCE...
"NEXT CAME THE MOST GRUELLING TWO HOURS OF MY LIFE--AS HERSHEY AND HIS FAMILY FOUGHT TO SAVE MY SON."
MOM AND DEAD
SURGERY FOR DUMIES
NAGGIE-- HOLD THAT BOOK UP TO THE LIGHT... METH--YOU PRE-HEAT THE OVEN--AH MEAN--READY THE ANESTHETIC!
" BY THE TIME IT WAS OVER, THE OTHERS HAD FOUND US. WE WERE TOGETHER WHEN WE HEARD THE NEWS.
...THE BOY WILL SURVIVE...
SIGH 'GUESS THAT MEANS RICE AND BEANS FOR EVERYONE--AGAIN!
" NEXT MORNING, WE RESUMED THE SEARCH FOR NO-SEE-UM.
..ME AND WAIL WILL WALK ALONG THESE LITTLE CIRCLES.
...THE TREES!
FERAL--YOU'LL FOLLOW THIS SQUIGGLY LINE....
...THE RIVER!
FROG

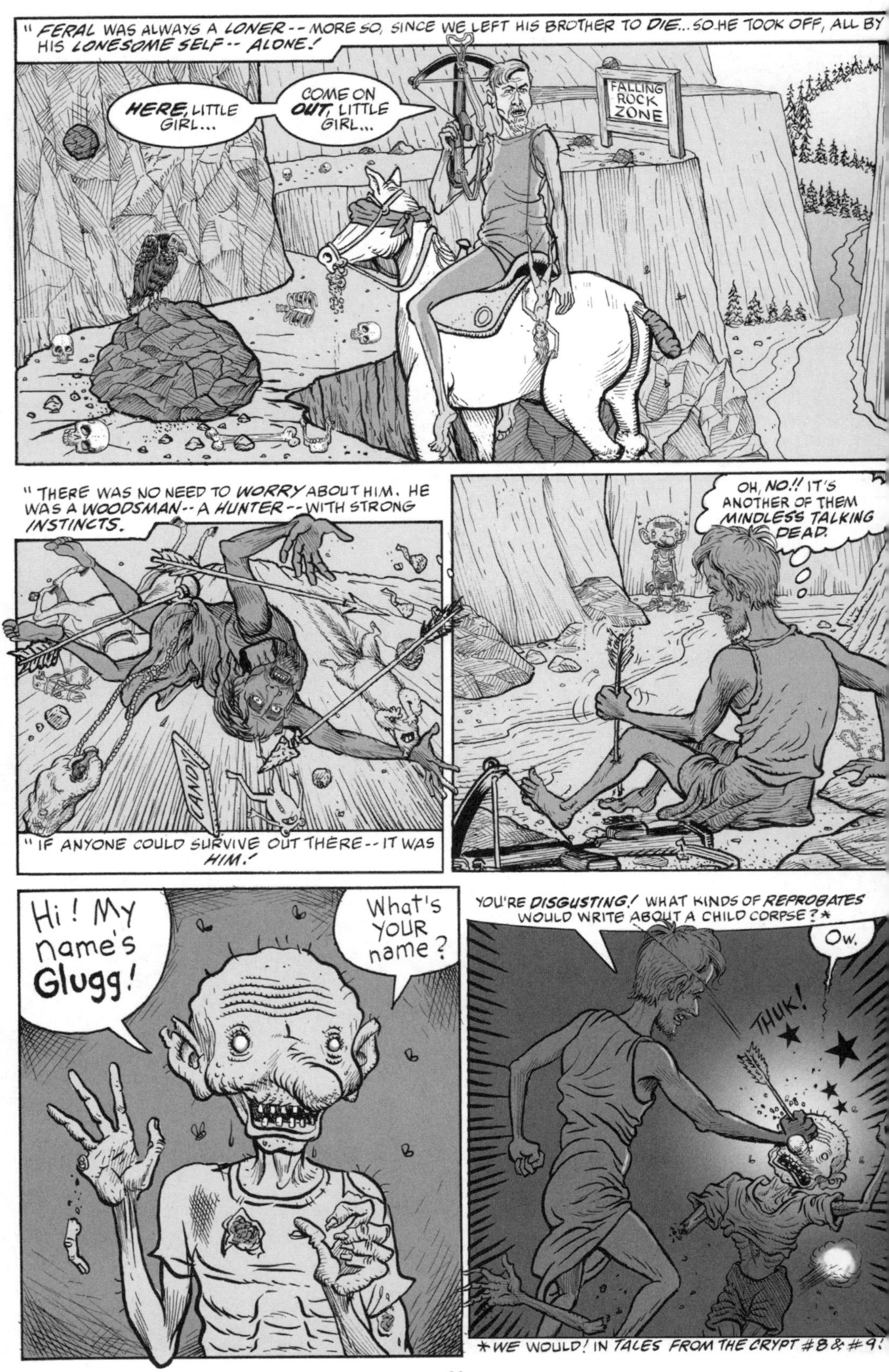

"FERAL WAS ALWAYS A LONER -- MORE SO, SINCE WE LEFT HIS BROTHER TO DIE... SO HE TOOK OFF, ALL BY HIS LONESOME SELF -- ALONE!
HERE, LITTLE GIRL...
COME ON OUT, LITTLE GIRL...
FALLING ROCK ZONE
"THERE WAS NO NEED TO WORRY ABOUT HIM. HE WAS A WOODSMAN -- A HUNTER -- WITH STRONG INSTINCTS.
CANDY
"IF ANYONE COULD SURVIVE OUT THERE -- IT WAS HIM!"
OH, NO!! IT'S ANOTHER OF THEM MINDLESS TALKING DEAD.
Hi! My name's Glugg!
What's YOUR name?
YOU'RE DISGUSTING! WHAT KINDS OF REPROBATES WOULD WRITE ABOUT A CHILD CORPSE?*
Ow.
THUK!
*WE WOULD! IN TALES FROM THE CRYPT #8 & #9!

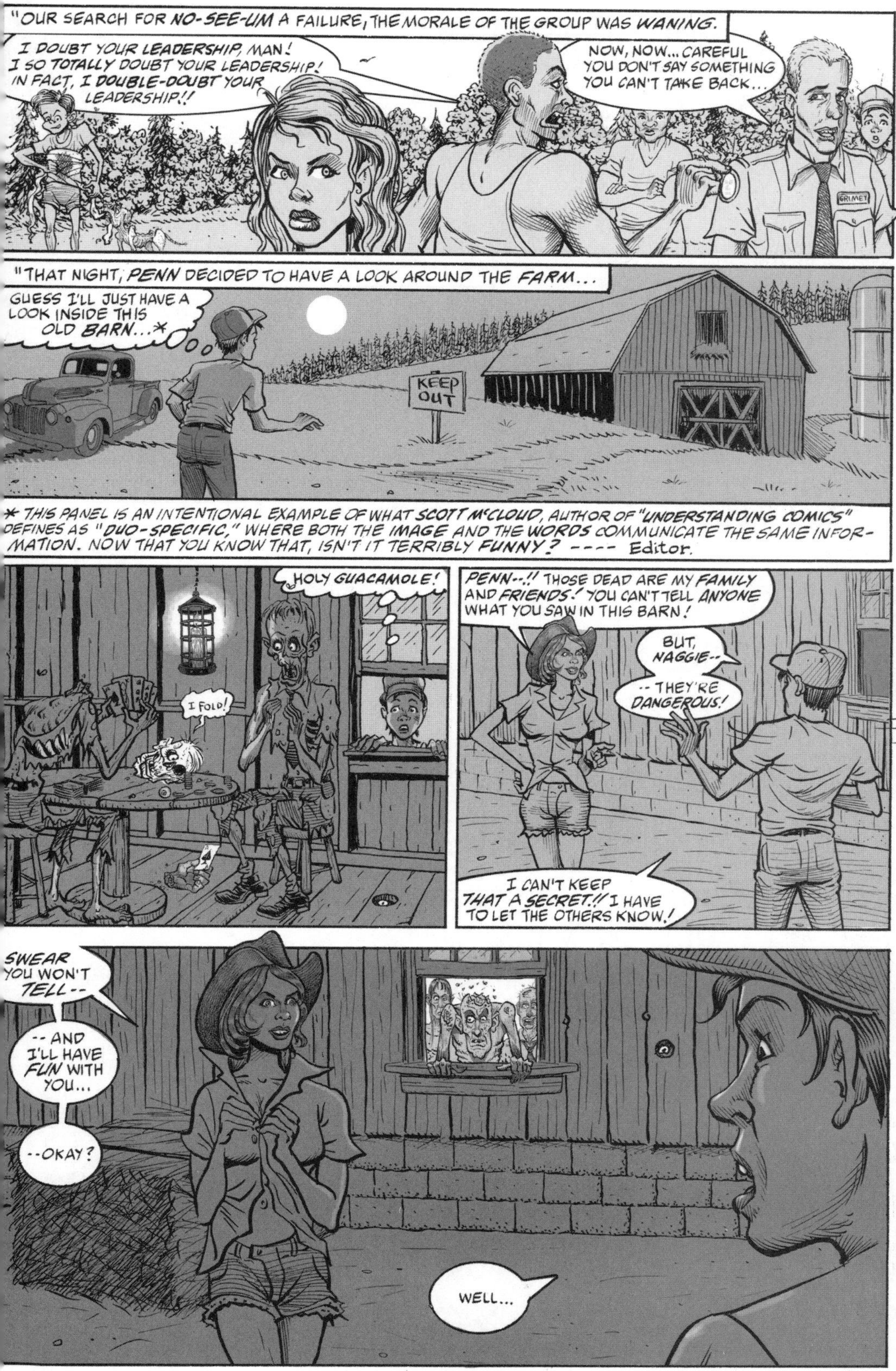
"OUR SEARCH FOR NO-SEE-UM A FAILURE, THE MORALE OF THE GROUP WAS WANING.
I DOUBT YOUR LEADERSHIP, MAN! I SO TOTALLY DOUBT YOUR LEADERSHIP! IN FACT, I DOUBLE-DOUBT YOUR LEADERSHIP!!
NOW, NOW... CAREFUL YOU DON'T SAY SOMETHING YOU CAN'T TAKE BACK...
GRIMEY
"THAT NIGHT, PENN DECIDED TO HAVE A LOOK AROUND THE FARM...
GUESS I'LL JUST HAVE A LOOK INSIDE THIS OLD BARN...*
KEEP OUT
* THIS PANEL IS AN INTENTIONAL EXAMPLE OF WHAT SCOTT McCLOUD, AUTHOR OF "UNDERSTANDING COMICS" DEFINES AS "DUO-SPECIFIC," WHERE BOTH THE IMAGE AND THE WORDS COMMUNICATE THE SAME INFORMATION. NOW THAT YOU KNOW THAT, ISN'T IT TERRIBLY FUNNY? ---- Editor.
HOLY GUACAMOLE!
I FOLD!
PENN--!! THOSE DEAD ARE MY FAMILY AND FRIENDS! YOU CAN'T TELL ANYONE WHAT YOU SAW IN THIS BARN!
BUT, NAGGIE--
-- THEY'RE DANGEROUS!
I CAN'T KEEP THAT A SECRET!! I HAVE TO LET THE OTHERS KNOW!
SWEAR YOU WON'T TELL--
-- AND I'LL HAVE FUN WITH YOU...
--OKAY?
WELL...

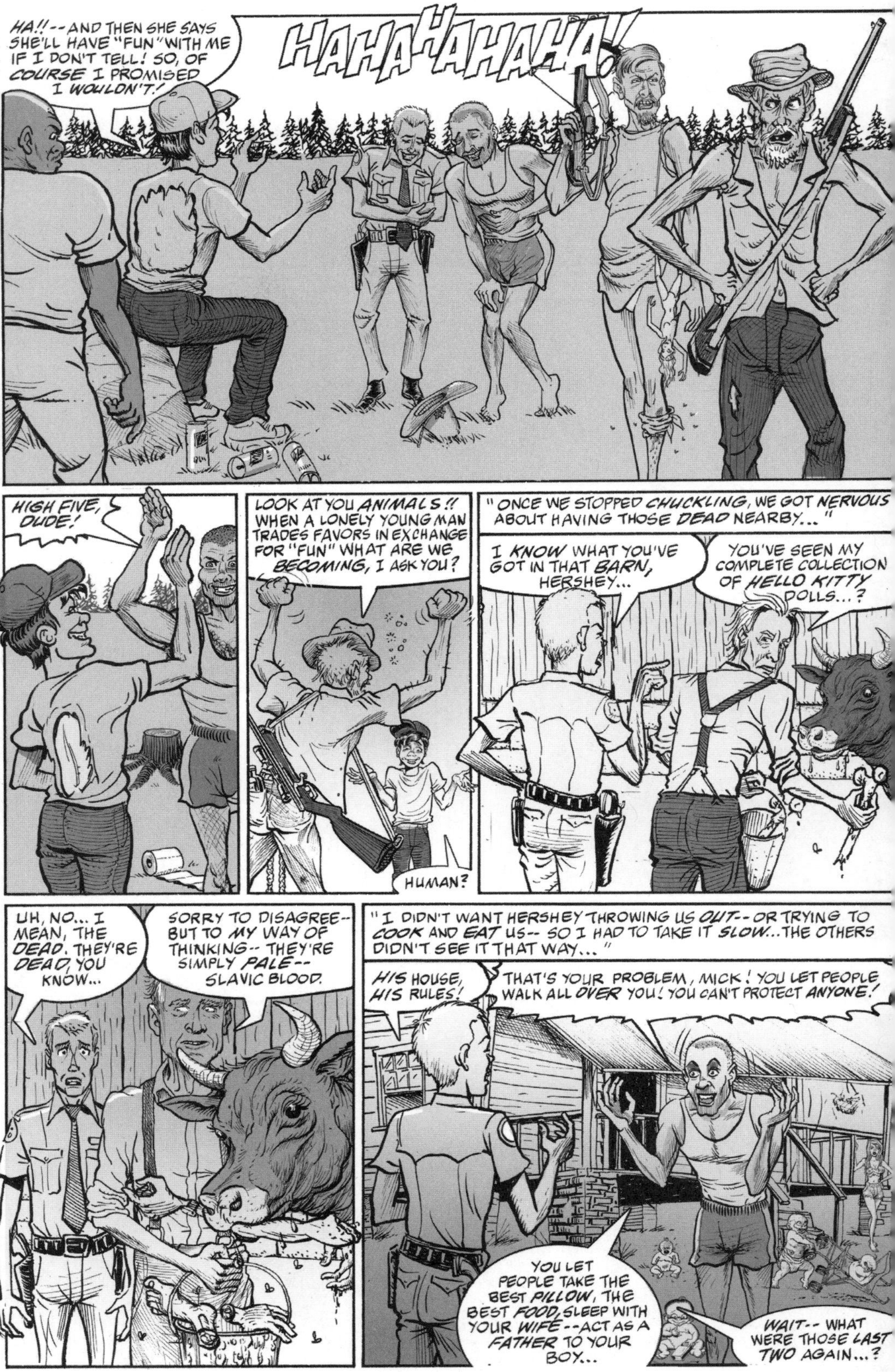
HA!! -- AND THEN SHE SAYS SHE'LL HAVE "FUN" WITH ME IF I DON'T TELL! SO, OF COURSE I PROMISED I WOULDN'T!
HAHAHAHAHAHA!
HIGH FIVE, DUDE!
LOOK AT YOU ANIMALS!! WHEN A LONELY YOUNG MAN TRADES FAVORS IN EXCHANGE FOR "FUN" WHAT ARE WE BECOMING, I ASK YOU?
HUMAN?
"ONCE WE STOPPED CHUCKLING, WE GOT NERVOUS ABOUT HAVING THOSE DEAD NEARBY..."
I KNOW WHAT YOU'VE GOT IN THAT BARN, HERSHEY...
YOU'VE SEEN MY COMPLETE COLLECTION OF HELLO KITTY DOLLS...?
UH, NO... I MEAN, THE DEAD. THEY'RE DEAD, YOU KNOW...
SORRY TO DISAGREE-- BUT TO MY WAY OF THINKING-- THEY'RE SIMPLY PALE-- SLAVIC BLOOD.
"I DIDN'T WANT HERSHEY THROWING US OUT-- OR TRYING TO COOK AND EAT US-- SO I HAD TO TAKE IT SLOW...THE OTHERS DIDN'T SEE IT THAT WAY..."
HIS HOUSE, HIS RULES!
THAT'S YOUR PROBLEM, MICK! YOU LET PEOPLE WALK ALL OVER YOU! YOU CAN'T PROTECT ANYONE!
YOU LET PEOPLE TAKE THE BEST PILLOW, THE BEST FOOD, SLEEP WITH YOUR WIFE--ACT AS A FATHER TO YOUR BOY...
WAIT-- WHAT WERE THOSE LAST TWO AGAIN...?

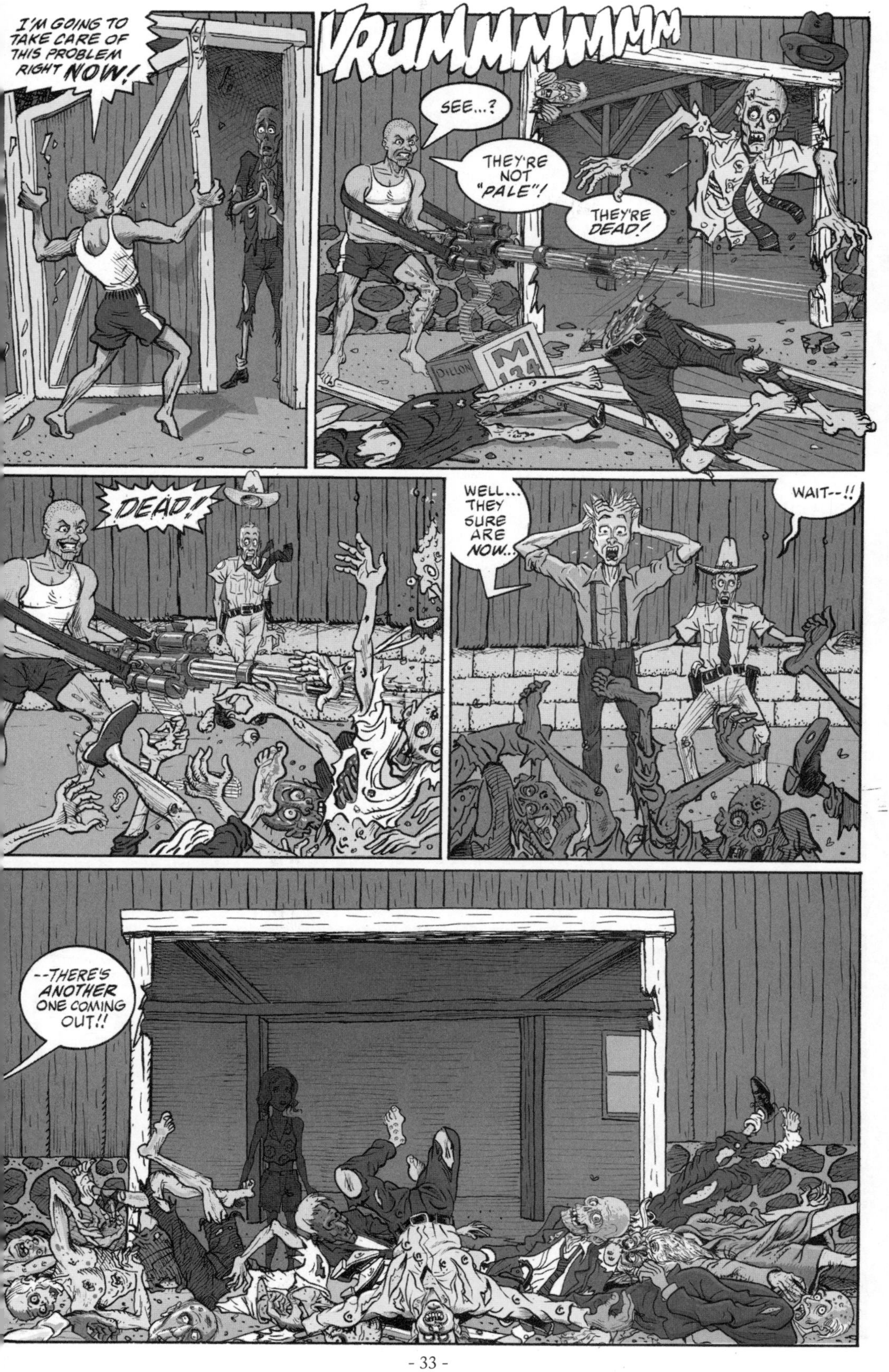
I'M GOING TO TAKE CARE OF THIS PROBLEM RIGHT NOW!
VRUMMMMMMM
SEE...?
THEY'RE NOT "PALE"!
THEY'RE DEAD!
M 134
DILLON
DEAD!
WELL... THEY SURE ARE NOW...
WAIT--!!
--THERE'S ANOTHER ONE COMING OUT!!

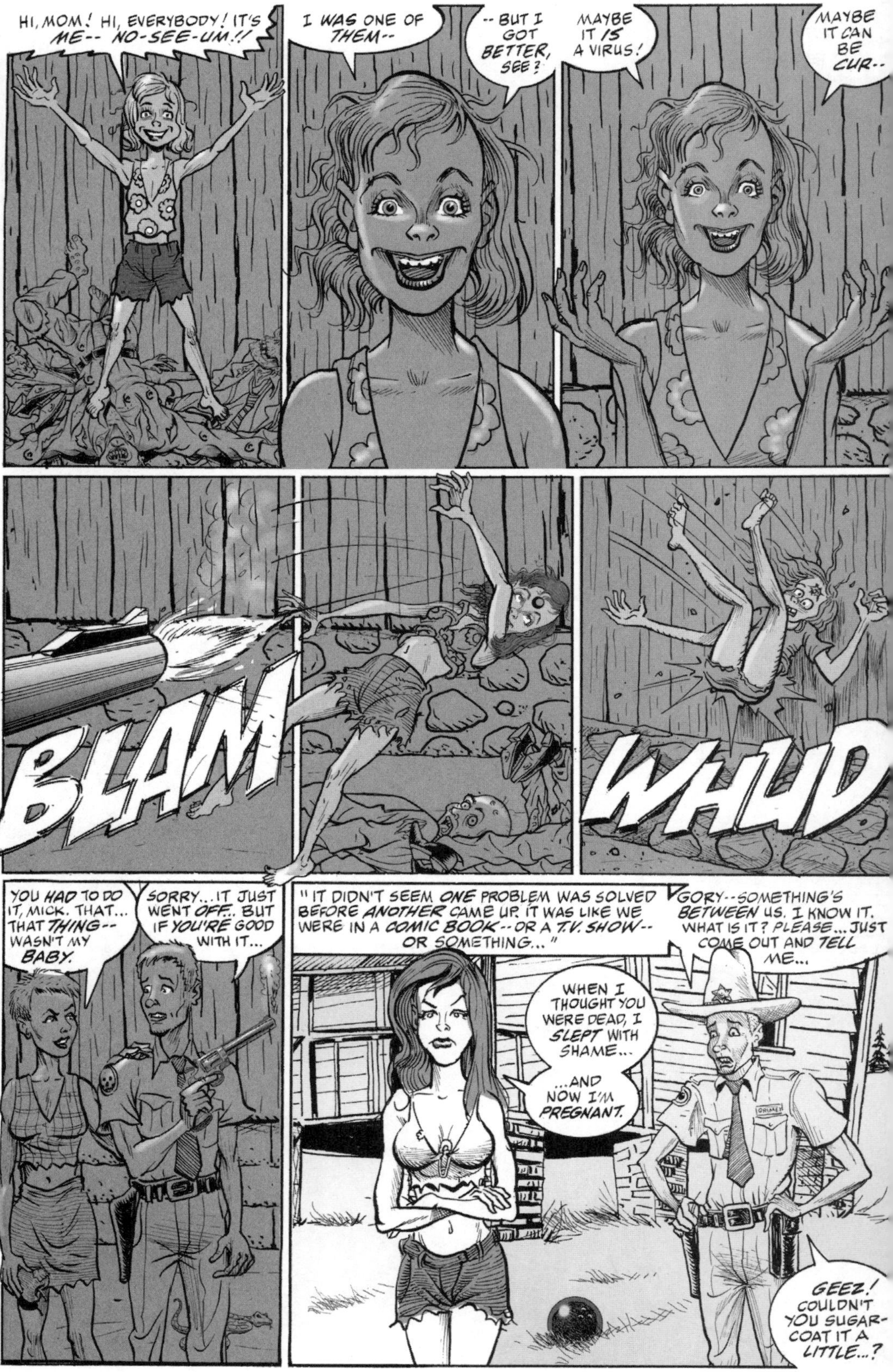
HI, MOM! HI, EVERYBODY! IT'S ME-- NO-SEE-UM!!
I WAS ONE OF THEM--
--BUT I GOT BETTER, SEE?
MAYBE IT IS A VIRUS!
MAYBE IT CAN BE CUR--
BLAM
WHUD
YOU HAD TO DO IT, MICK. THAT... THAT THING-- WASN'T MY BABY.
SORRY... IT JUST WENT OFF... BUT IF YOU'RE GOOD WITH IT...
"IT DIDN'T SEEM ONE PROBLEM WAS SOLVED BEFORE ANOTHER CAME UP. IT WAS LIKE WE WERE IN A COMIC BOOK--OR A T.V. SHOW--OR SOMETHING..."
GORY--SOMETHING'S BETWEEN US. I KNOW IT. WHAT IS IT? PLEASE... JUST COME OUT AND TELL ME...
WHEN I THOUGHT YOU WERE DEAD, I SLEPT WITH SHAME...
...AND NOW I'M PREGNANT.
GEEZ! COULDN'T YOU SUGAR-COAT IT A LITTLE...?

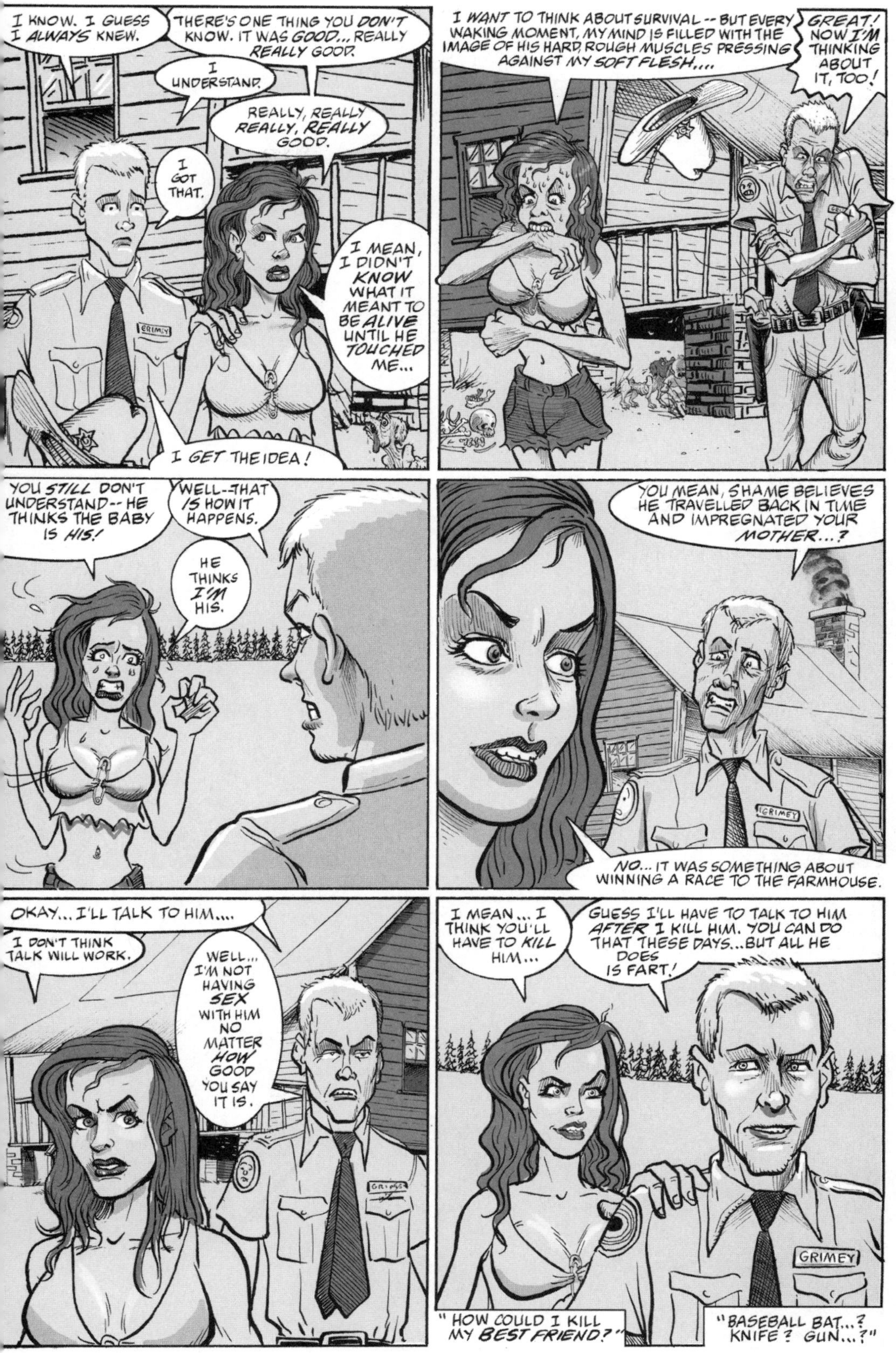
I KNOW. I GUESS I ALWAYS KNEW.
THERE'S ONE THING YOU DON'T KNOW. IT WAS GOOD..., REALLY REALLY GOOD.
I UNDERSTAND.
REALLY, REALLY REALLY, REALLY GOOD.
I GOT THAT.
I MEAN, I DIDN'T KNOW WHAT IT MEANT TO BE ALIVE UNTIL HE TOUCHED ME...
I GET THE IDEA!
I WANT TO THINK ABOUT SURVIVAL -- BUT EVERY WAKING MOMENT, MY MIND IS FILLED WITH THE IMAGE OF HIS HARD ROUGH MUSCLES PRESSING AGAINST MY SOFT FLESH....
GREAT! NOW I'M THINKING ABOUT IT, TOO!
YOU STILL DON'T UNDERSTAND-- HE THINKS THE BABY IS HIS!
WELL--THAT IS HOW IT HAPPENS.
HE THINKS I'M HIS.
YOU MEAN, SHAME BELIEVES HE TRAVELLED BACK IN TIME AND IMPREGNATED YOUR MOTHER...?
GRIMEY
NO... IT WAS SOMETHING ABOUT WINNING A RACE TO THE FARMHOUSE.
OKAY... I'LL TALK TO HIM....
I DON'T THINK TALK WILL WORK.
WELL... I'M NOT HAVING SEX WITH HIM NO MATTER HOW GOOD YOU SAY IT IS.
I MEAN... I THINK YOU'LL HAVE TO KILL HIM...
GUESS I'LL HAVE TO TALK TO HIM AFTER I KILL HIM. YOU CAN DO THAT THESE DAYS...BUT ALL HE DOES IS FART!
GRIMEY
"HOW COULD I KILL MY BEST FRIEND?"
"BASEBALL BAT...? KNIFE? GUN...?"

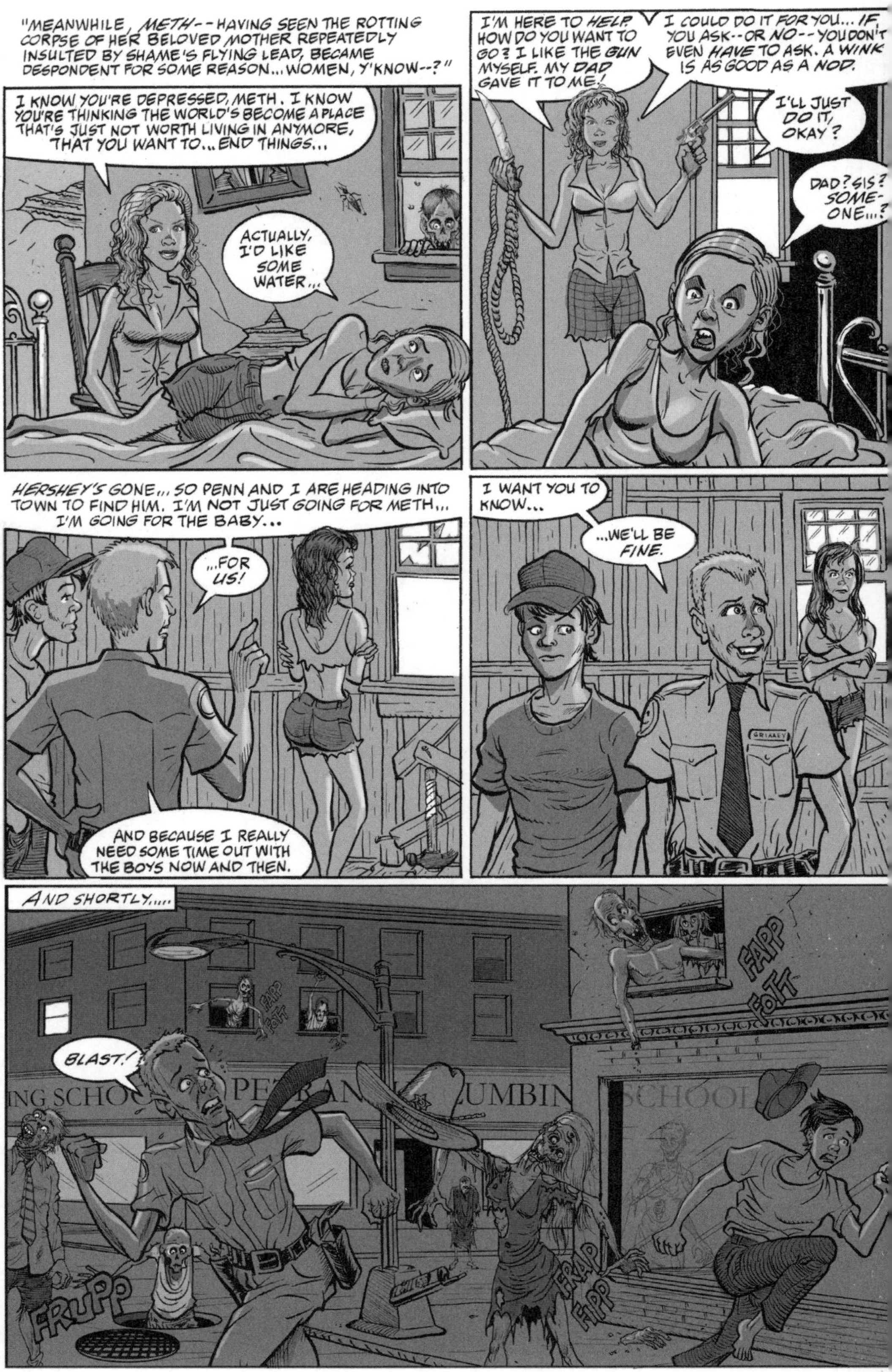
"MEANWHILE, METH--HAVING SEEN THE ROTTING CORPSE OF HER BELOVED MOTHER REPEATEDLY INSULTED BY SHAME'S FLYING LEAD, BECAME DESPONDENT FOR SOME REASON... WOMEN, Y'KNOW--?"
I KNOW YOU'RE DEPRESSED, METH. I KNOW YOU'RE THINKING THE WORLD'S BECOME A PLACE THAT'S JUST NOT WORTH LIVING IN ANYMORE, THAT YOU WANT TO... END THINGS...
ACTUALLY, I'D LIKE SOME WATER...
I'M HERE TO HELP. HOW DO YOU WANT TO GO? I LIKE THE GUN MYSELF. MY DAD GAVE IT TO ME!
I COULD DO IT FOR YOU... IF YOU ASK--OR NO--YOU DON'T EVEN HAVE TO ASK. A WINK IS AS GOOD AS A NOD.
I'LL JUST DO IT, OKAY?
DAD? SIS? SOME-ONE...?
HERSHEY'S GONE... SO PENN AND I ARE HEADING INTO TOWN TO FIND HIM. I'M NOT JUST GOING FOR METH... I'M GOING FOR THE BABY...
...FOR US!
AND BECAUSE I REALLY NEED SOME TIME OUT WITH THE BOYS NOW AND THEN.
I WANT YOU TO KNOW...
...WE'LL BE FINE.
GRIMEY
AND SHORTLY.....
FAPP
FOTT
FAPP
FOTT
BLAST!
ING SCHOO
PET
UMBIN
SCHOO
FRUPP
FRAPP
FAPP

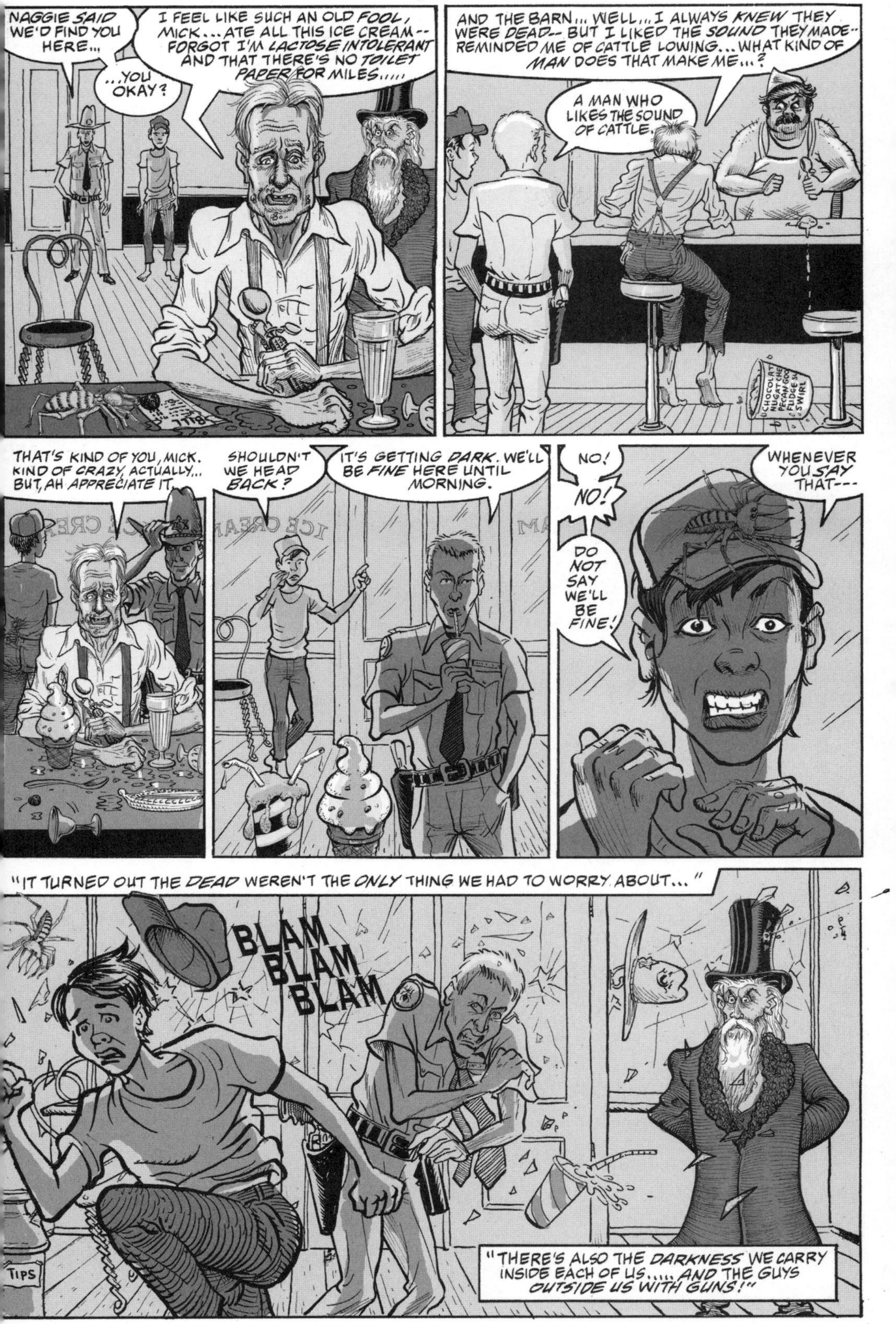
NAGGIE SAID WE'D FIND YOU HERE...
...YOU OKAY?
I FEEL LIKE SUCH AN OLD FOOL, MICK... ATE ALL THIS ICE CREAM-- FORGOT I'M LACTOSE INTOLERANT AND THAT THERE'S NO TOILET PAPER FOR MILES.....
BILL
AND THE BARN... WELL... I ALWAYS KNEW THEY WERE DEAD-- BUT I LIKED THE SOUND THEY MADE.. REMINDED ME OF CATTLE LOWING... WHAT KIND OF MAN DOES THAT MAKE ME...?
A MAN WHO LIKES THE SOUND OF CATTLE.
CHOCOLATE NUGAT PECAN FUDGE SWIRL
THAT'S KIND OF YOU, MICK. KIND OF CRAZY, ACTUALLY... BUT, AH APPRECIATE IT.
SHOULDN'T WE HEAD BACK?
IT'S GETTING DARK. WE'LL BE FINE HERE UNTIL MORNING.
ICE CREAM
NO!
NO!
DO NOT SAY WE'LL BE FINE!
WHENEVER YOU SAY THAT---
"IT TURNED OUT THE DEAD WEREN'T THE ONLY THING WE HAD TO WORRY ABOUT..."
BLAM BLAM BLAM
TIPS
"THERE'S ALSO THE DARKNESS WE CARRY INSIDE EACH OF US..... AND THE GUYS OUTSIDE US WITH GUNS!"

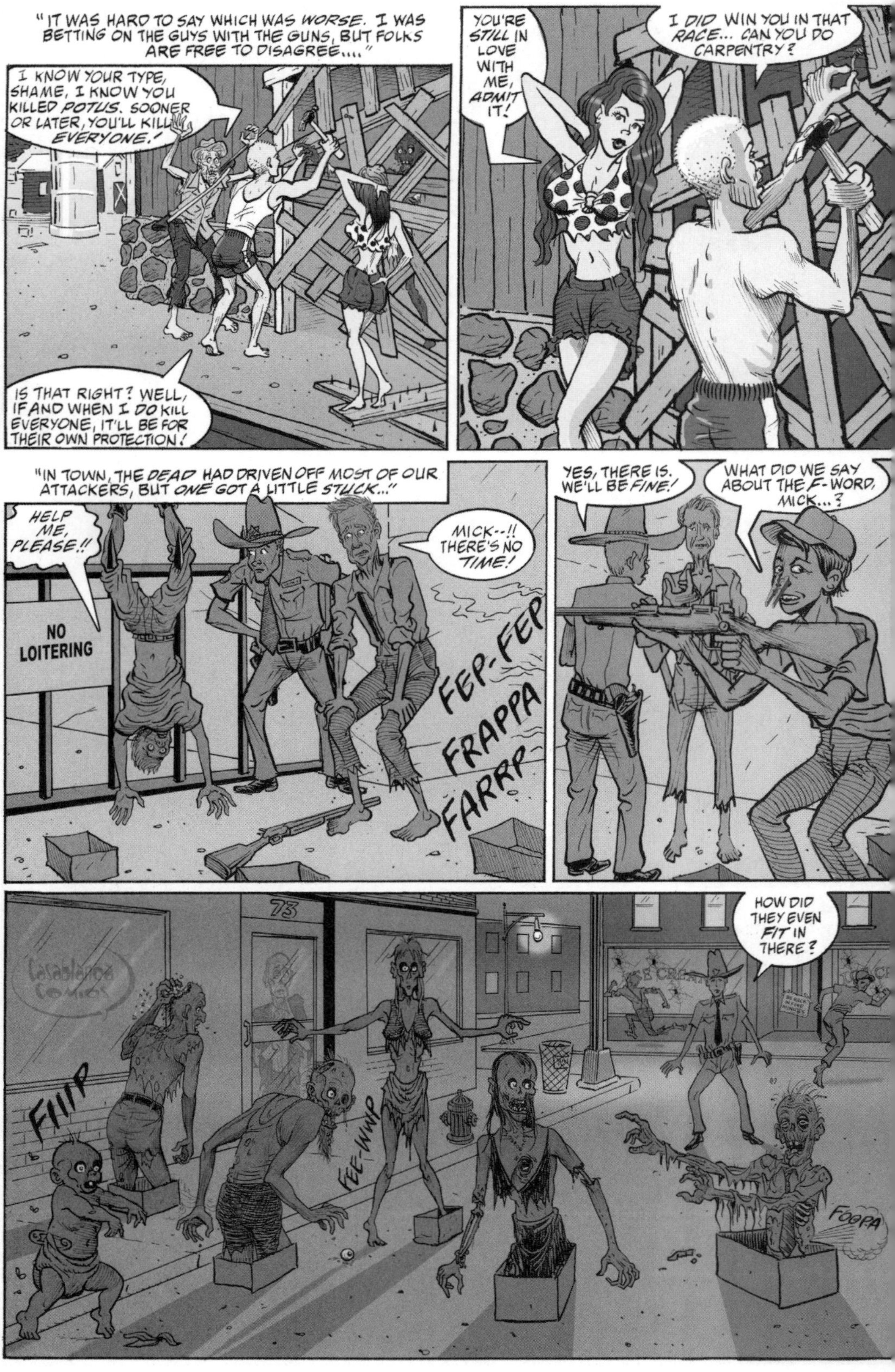
"IT WAS HARD TO SAY WHICH WAS WORSE. I WAS BETTING ON THE GUYS WITH THE GUNS, BUT FOLKS ARE FREE TO DISAGREE...."
I KNOW YOUR TYPE, SHAME, I KNOW YOU KILLED POTUS. SOONER OR LATER, YOU'LL KILL EVERYONE!
IS THAT RIGHT? WELL, IF AND WHEN I DO KILL EVERYONE, IT'LL BE FOR THEIR OWN PROTECTION!
YOU'RE STILL IN LOVE WITH ME, ADMIT IT!
I DID WIN YOU IN THAT RACE... CAN YOU DO CARPENTRY?
"IN TOWN, THE DEAD HAD DRIVEN OFF MOST OF OUR ATTACKERS, BUT ONE GOT A LITTLE STUCK..."
HELP ME, PLEASE!!
NO LOITERING
MICK--!! THERE'S NO TIME!
FEP-FEP
FRAPPA
FARRP
YES, THERE IS. WE'LL BE FINE!
WHAT DID WE SAY ABOUT THE F-WORD, MICK...?
73
HOW DID THEY EVEN FIT IN THERE?
FIIIP
FEE-WWP
FOOPA

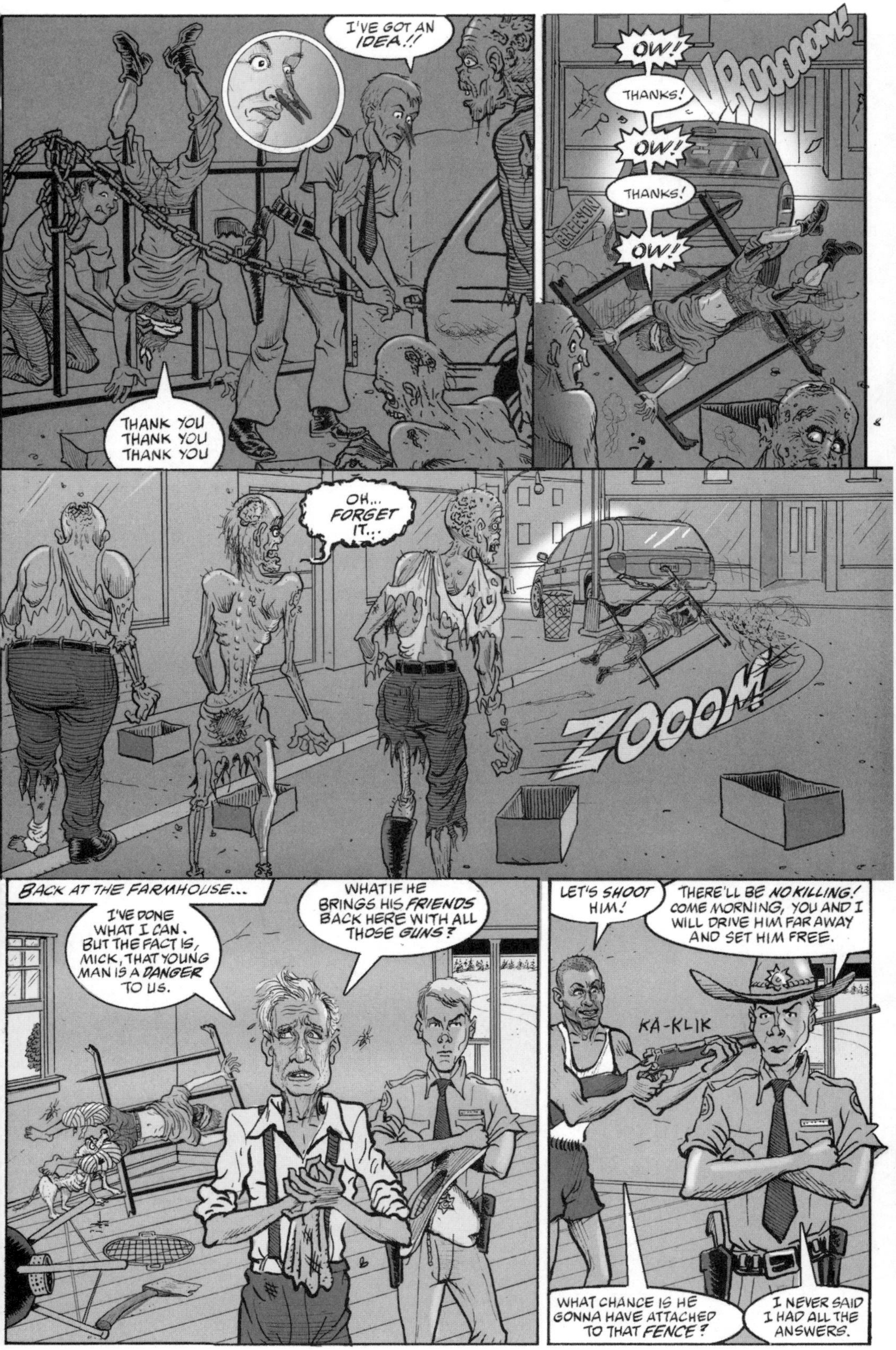
I'VE GOT AN IDEA!!
THANK YOU THANK YOU THANK YOU
OW!!
THANKS!
OW!!
THANKS!
OW!!
VROOOOOOM!
GREGSON
OH... FORGET IT...
ZOOOM!
BACK AT THE FARMHOUSE...
I'VE DONE WHAT I CAN. BUT THE FACT IS, MICK, THAT YOUNG MAN IS A DANGER TO US.
WHAT IF HE BRINGS HIS FRIENDS BACK HERE WITH ALL THOSE GUNS?
LET'S SHOOT HIM!
THERE'LL BE NO KILLING! COME MORNING, YOU AND I WILL DRIVE HIM FAR AWAY AND SET HIM FREE.
KA-KLIK
WHAT CHANCE IS HE GONNA HAVE ATTACHED TO THAT FENCE?
I NEVER SAID I HAD ALL THE ANSWERS.

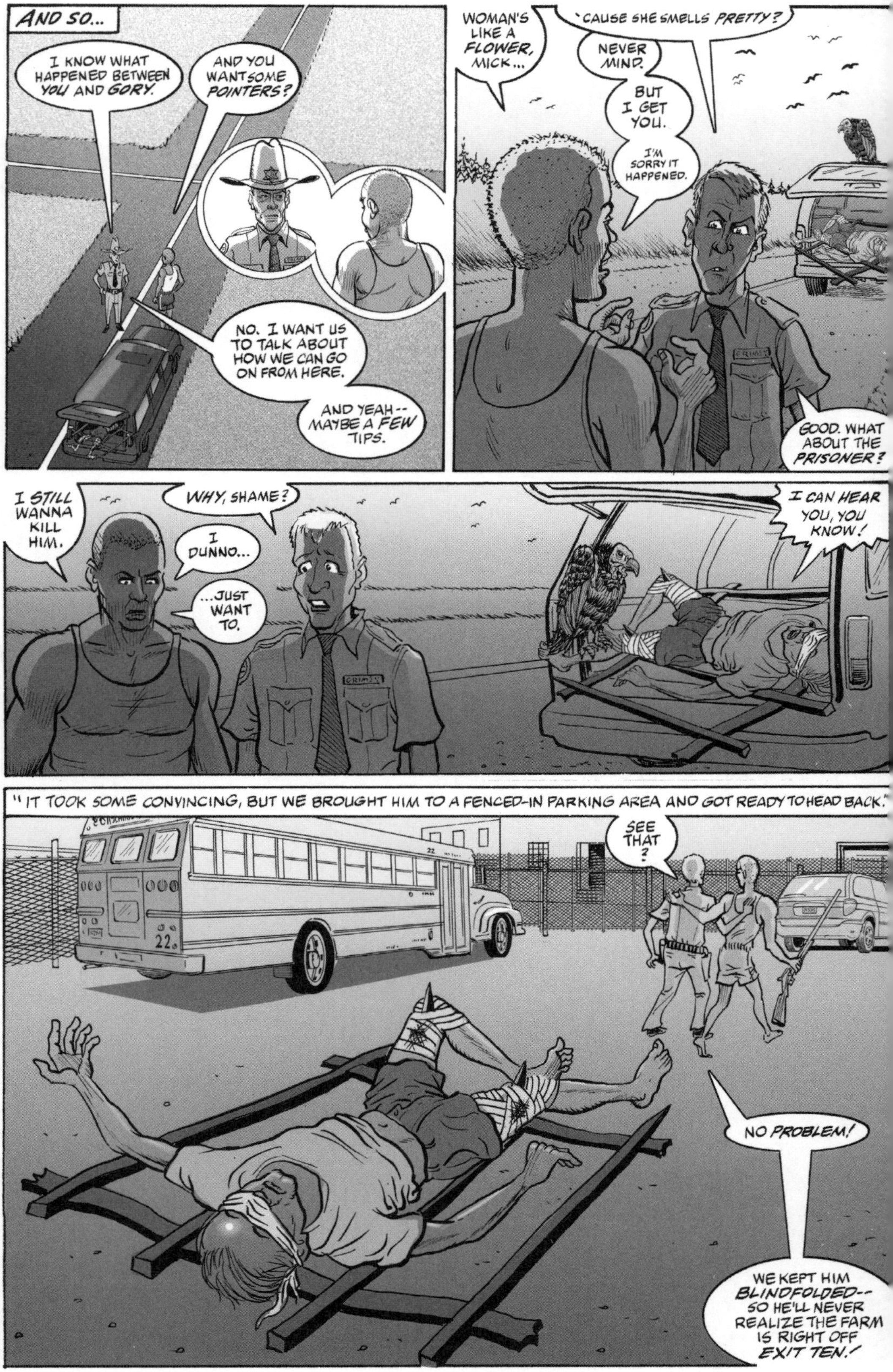
AND SO...
I KNOW WHAT HAPPENED BETWEEN YOU AND GORY.
AND YOU WANT SOME POINTERS?
NO. I WANT US TO TALK ABOUT HOW WE CAN GO ON FROM HERE.
AND YEAH-- MAYBE A FEW TIPS.
WOMAN'S LIKE A FLOWER, MICK...
'CAUSE SHE SMELLS PRETTY?
NEVER MIND.
BUT I GET YOU.
I'M SORRY IT HAPPENED.
GOOD. WHAT ABOUT THE PRISONER?
I STILL WANNA KILL HIM.
WHY, SHAME?
I DUNNO...
...JUST WANT TO.
I CAN HEAR YOU, YOU KNOW!
"IT TOOK SOME CONVINCING, BUT WE BROUGHT HIM TO A FENCED-IN PARKING AREA AND GOT READY TO HEAD BACK."
SEE THAT?
NO PROBLEM!
WE KEPT HIM BLINDFOLDED-- SO HE'LL NEVER REALIZE THE FARM IS RIGHT OFF EXIT TEN!

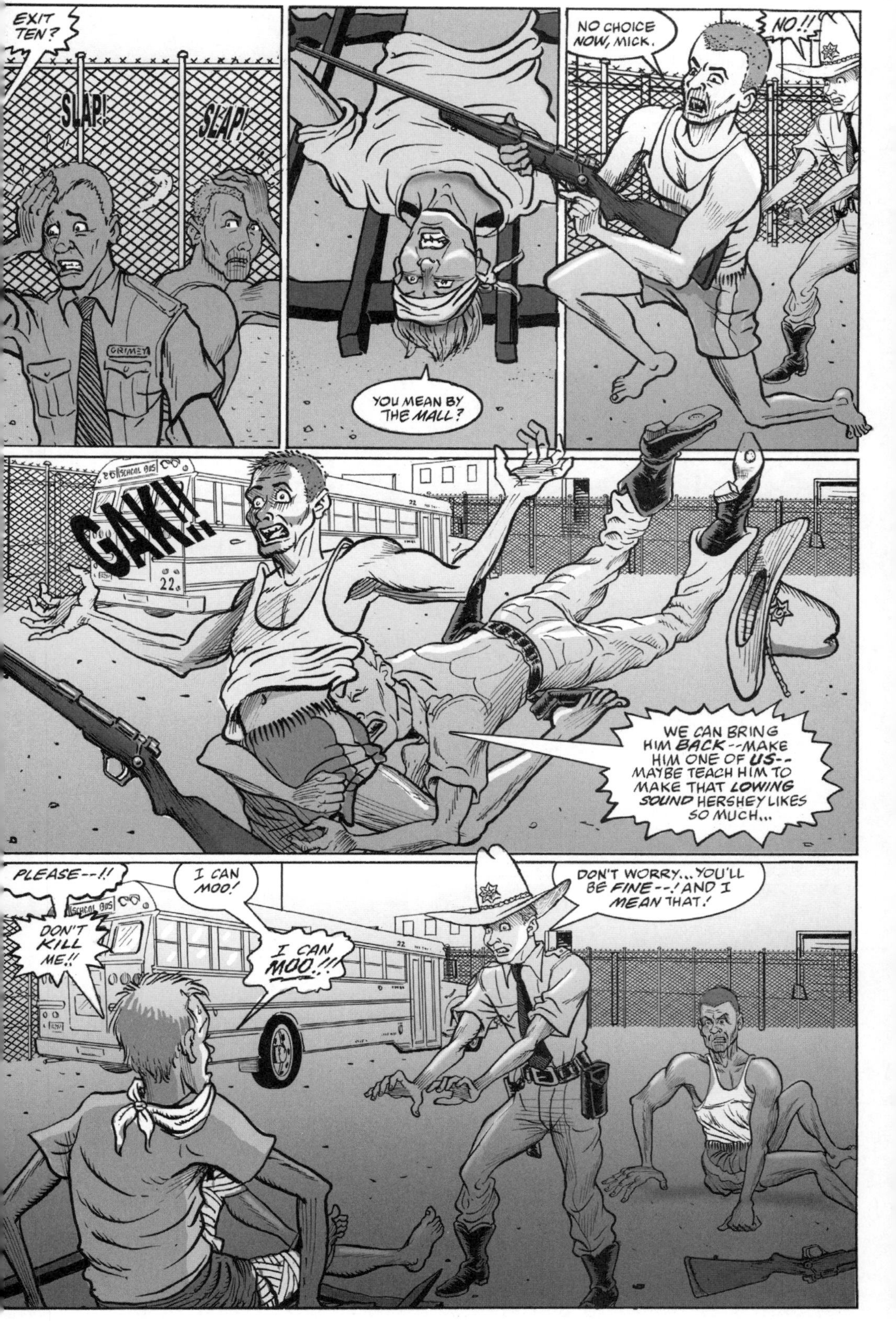

EXIT TEN?
SLAP!
SLAP!
GRIMEY
YOU MEAN BY THE MALL?
NO CHOICE NOW, MICK.
NO!!
GAK!!
WE CAN BRING HIM BACK--MAKE HIM ONE OF US--MAYBE TEACH HIM TO MAKE THAT LOWING SOUND HERSHEY LIKES SO MUCH...
PLEASE--!!
DON'T KILL ME!!
I CAN MOO!
I CAN MOO!!!
DON'T WORRY...YOU'LL BE FINE--! AND I MEAN THAT!

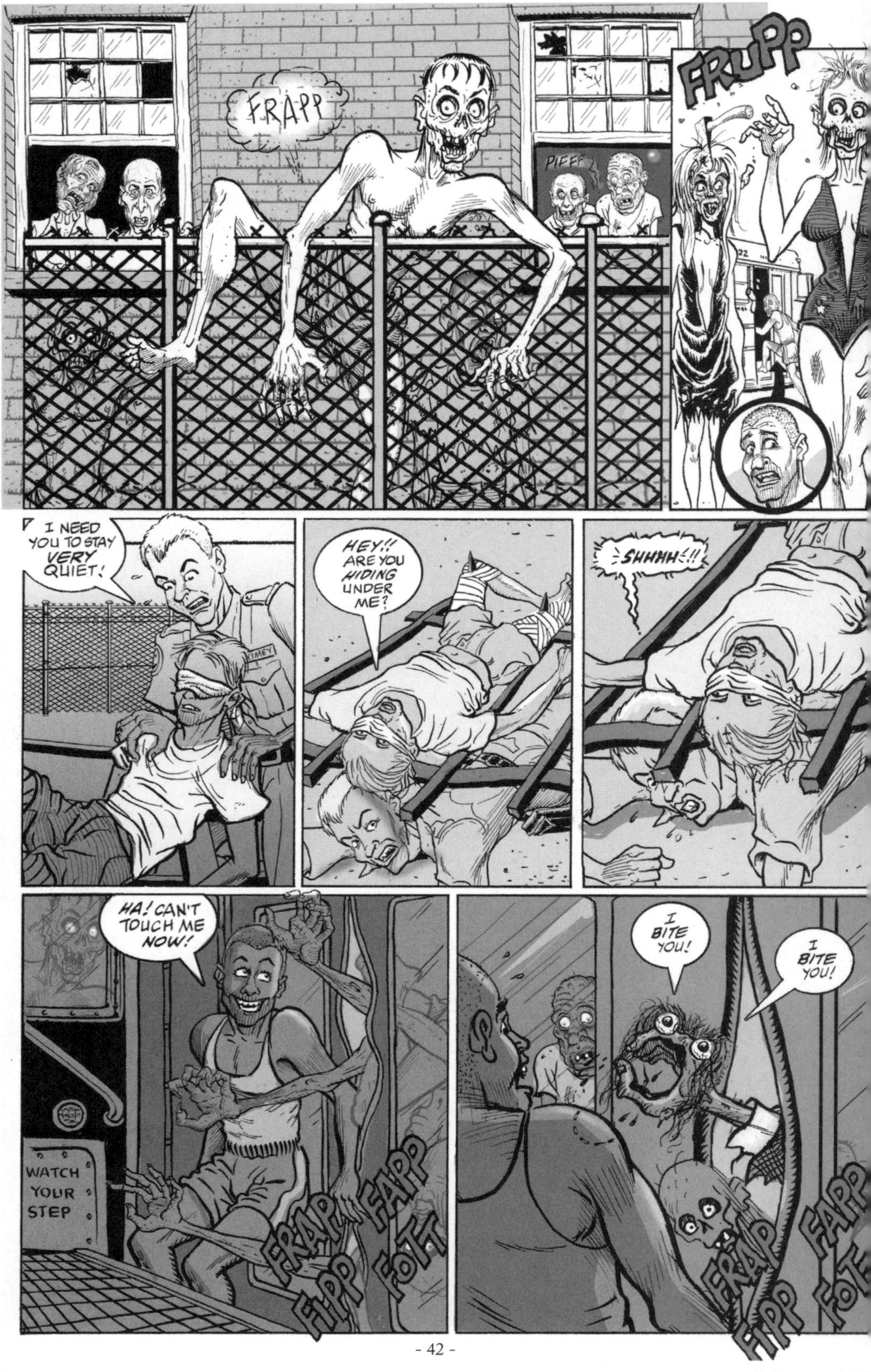

FRAPP
PIFFF
FRUPP
I NEED YOU TO STAY VERY QUIET!
HEY!! ARE YOU HIDING UNDER ME?
SHHHH!!
HA! CAN'T TOUCH ME NOW!
WATCH YOUR STEP
FRAP FIPP FAPP FOTT
I BITE YOU!
I BITE YOU!
FRAP FIPP FAPP FOTT

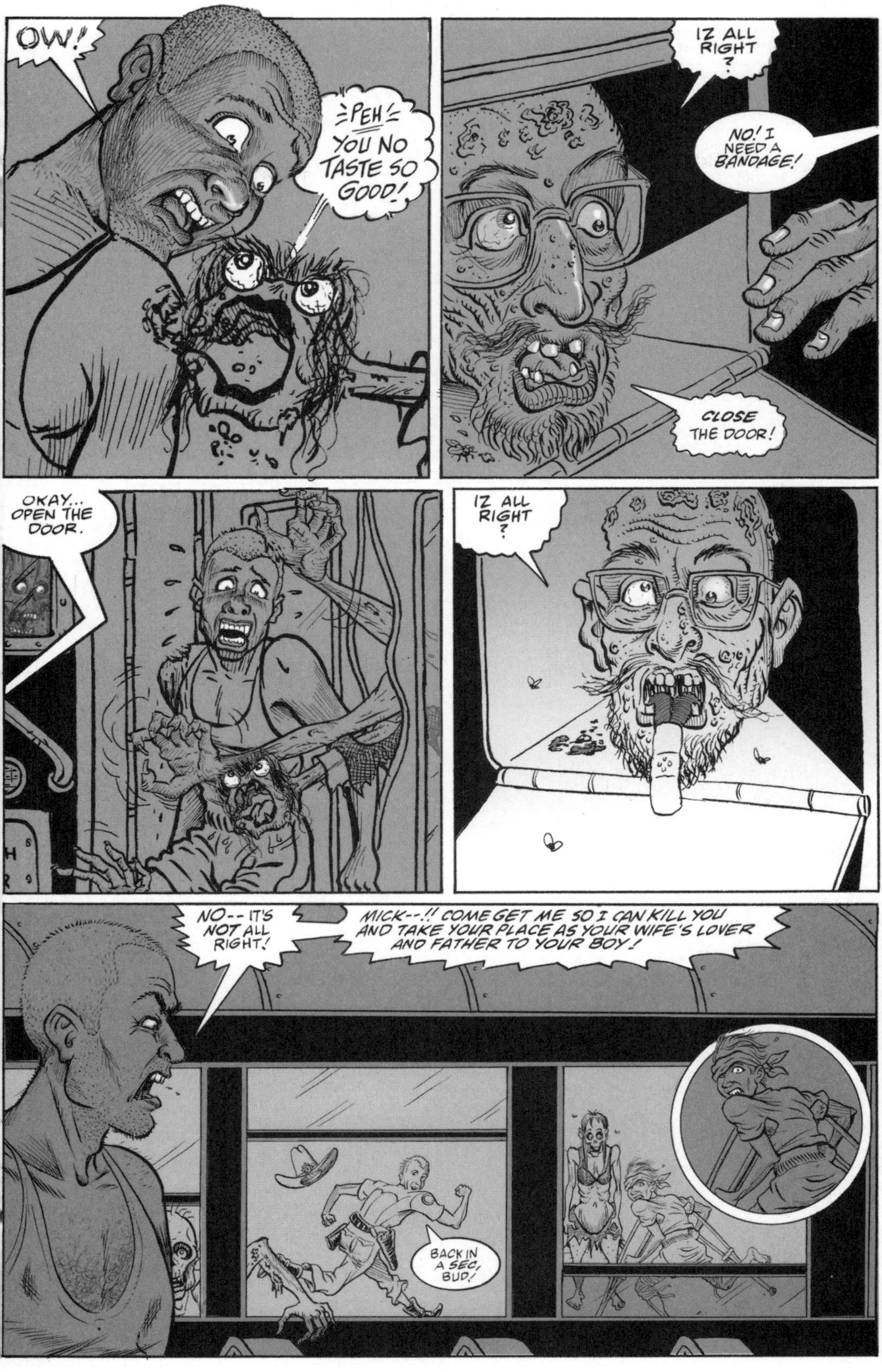
OW!
PEH
YOU NO TASTE SO GOOD!
IZ ALL RIGHT ?
NO! I NEED A BANDAGE!
CLOSE THE DOOR!
OKAY... OPEN THE DOOR.
IZ ALL RIGHT ?
NO-- IT'S NOT ALL RIGHT!
MICK--!! COME GET ME SO I CAN KILL YOU AND TAKE YOUR PLACE AS YOUR WIFE'S LOVER AND FATHER TO YOUR BOY!
BACK IN A SEC, BUD!

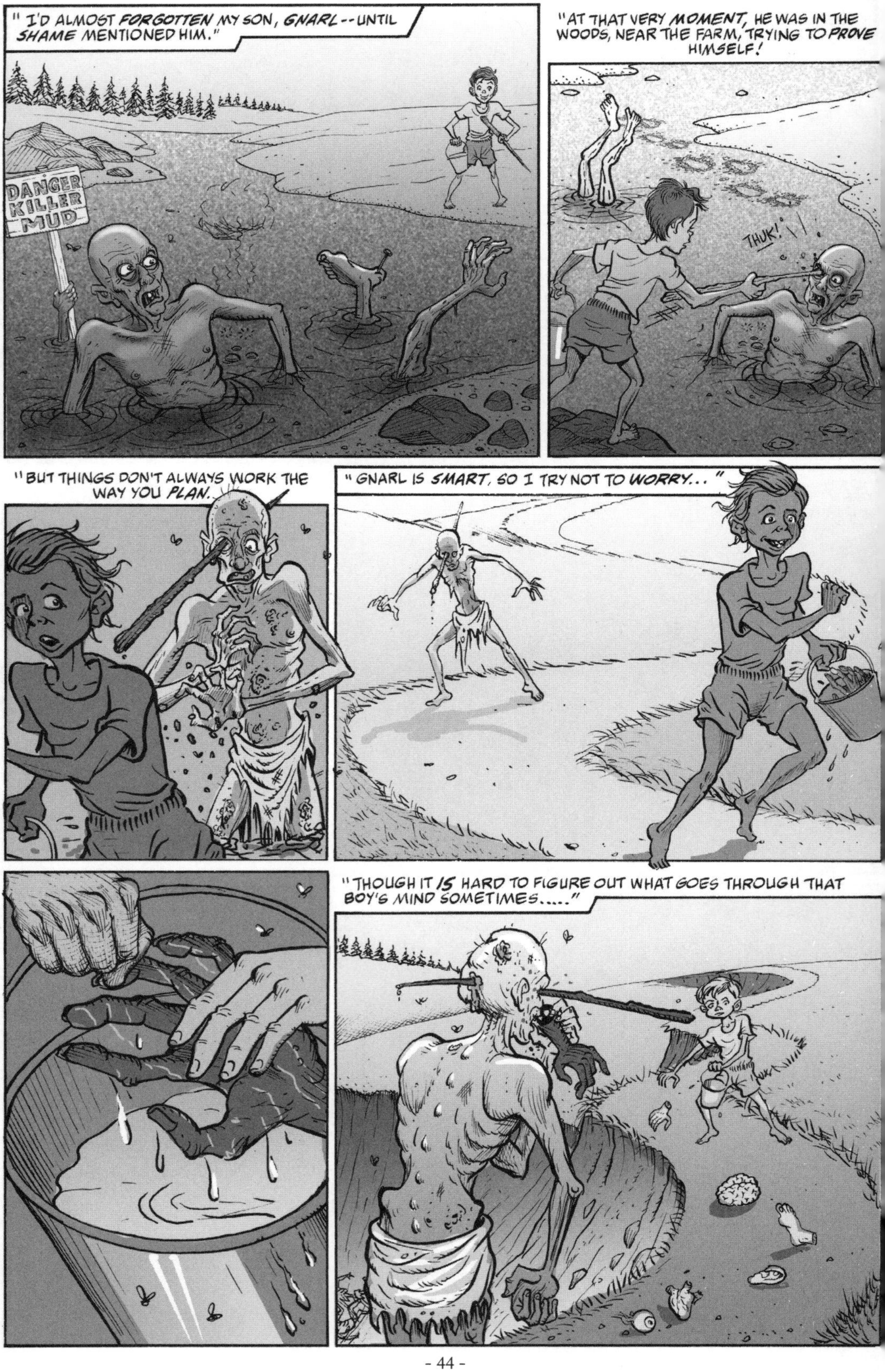
"I'D ALMOST FORGOTTEN MY SON, GNARL--UNTIL SHAME MENTIONED HIM."
DANGER KILLER MUD
"AT THAT VERY MOMENT, HE WAS IN THE WOODS, NEAR THE FARM, TRYING TO PROVE HIMSELF!
THUK!
"BUT THINGS DON'T ALWAYS WORK THE WAY YOU PLAN.
"GNARL IS SMART, SO I TRY NOT TO WORRY..."
"THOUGH IT IS HARD TO FIGURE OUT WHAT GOES THROUGH THAT BOY'S MIND SOMETIMES....."

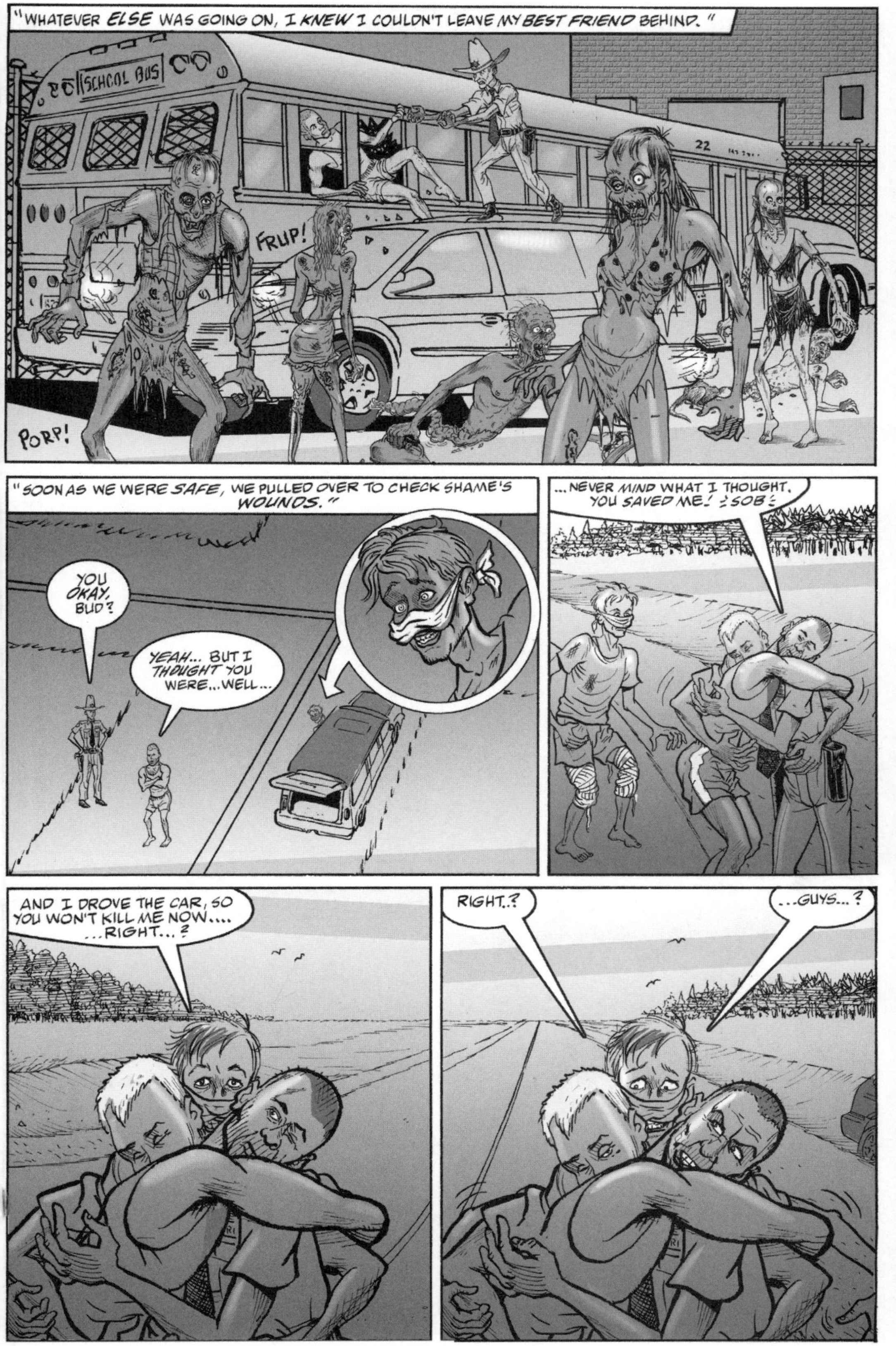
"WHATEVER ELSE WAS GOING ON, I KNEW I COULDN'T LEAVE MY BEST FRIEND BEHIND."
SCHOOL BUS
22
FRUP!
PORP!
"SOON AS WE WERE SAFE, WE PULLED OVER TO CHECK SHAME'S WOUNDS."
YOU OKAY, BUD?
YEAH... BUT I THOUGHT YOU WERE... WELL...
...NEVER MIND WHAT I THOUGHT. YOU SAVED ME! ¿SOB¿
AND I DROVE THE CAR, SO YOU WON'T KILL ME NOW.... ...RIGHT...?
RIGHT..?
...GUYS...?

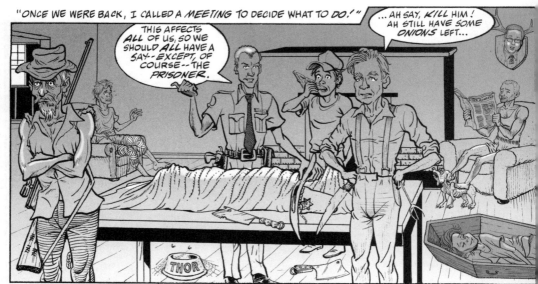

"ONCE WE WERE BACK, I CALLED A *MEETING* TO DECIDE WHAT TO *DO!*"

THIS AFFECTS *ALL* OF US, SO WE SHOULD *ALL* HAVE A SAY--EXCEPT, OF COURSE--THE *PRISONER.*

...AH SAY, *KILL* HIM! AH STILL HAVE SOME *ONIONS* LEFT...

WE'RE GONNA JUST MURDER HIM BECAUSE HE *MIGHT* ATTACK US? WHAT DOES *THAT* MAKE *US??*

THAT'S WHY WE INVADED *IRAQ,* ISN'T IT?

HONESTLY, WAIL--NEXT YOU'LL TELL US TO TAKE DOWN THOSE CARTOONS WE MADE INSULTING ISLAM

I WON'T BE A *PART* OF IT! I DON'T CARE *HOW* VULNERABLE WALKING ALONE OUTSIDE MAKES ME...

CHANGED MY MIND! CHANGED MY MIND!

KLIK KLIK KLIK

BRAP

I ALWAYS WONDERED WHAT WAS IN THERE.....

- 46 -

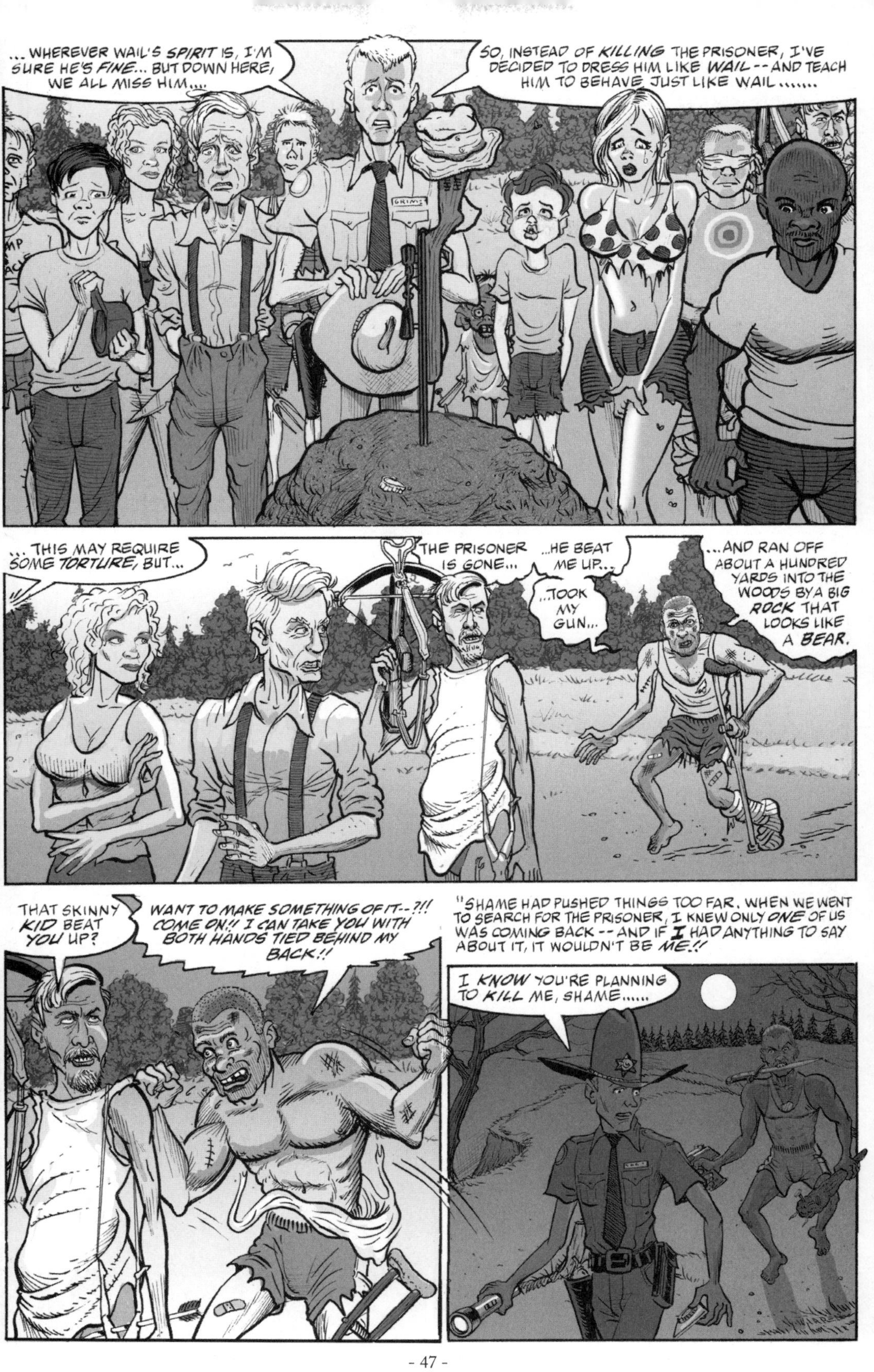

... WHEREVER WAIL'S SPIRIT IS, I'M SURE HE'S FINE... BUT DOWN HERE, WE ALL MISS HIM.....
SO, INSTEAD OF KILLING THE PRISONER, I'VE DECIDED TO DRESS HIM LIKE WAIL -- AND TEACH HIM TO BEHAVE JUST LIKE WAIL.......
... THIS MAY REQUIRE SOME TORTURE, BUT...
THE PRISONER IS GONE...
...HE BEAT ME UP...
...TOOK MY GUN...
...AND RAN OFF ABOUT A HUNDRED YARDS INTO THE WOODS BY A BIG ROCK THAT LOOKS LIKE A BEAR.
THAT SKINNY KID BEAT YOU UP?
WANT TO MAKE SOMETHING OF IT--?!! COME ON!! I CAN TAKE YOU WITH BOTH HANDS TIED BEHIND MY BACK!!
"SHAME HAD PUSHED THINGS TOO FAR. WHEN WE WENT TO SEARCH FOR THE PRISONER, I KNEW ONLY ONE OF US WAS COMING BACK -- AND IF I HAD ANYTHING TO SAY ABOUT IT, IT WOULDN'T BE ME.!!
I KNOW YOU'RE PLANNING TO KILL ME, SHAME......

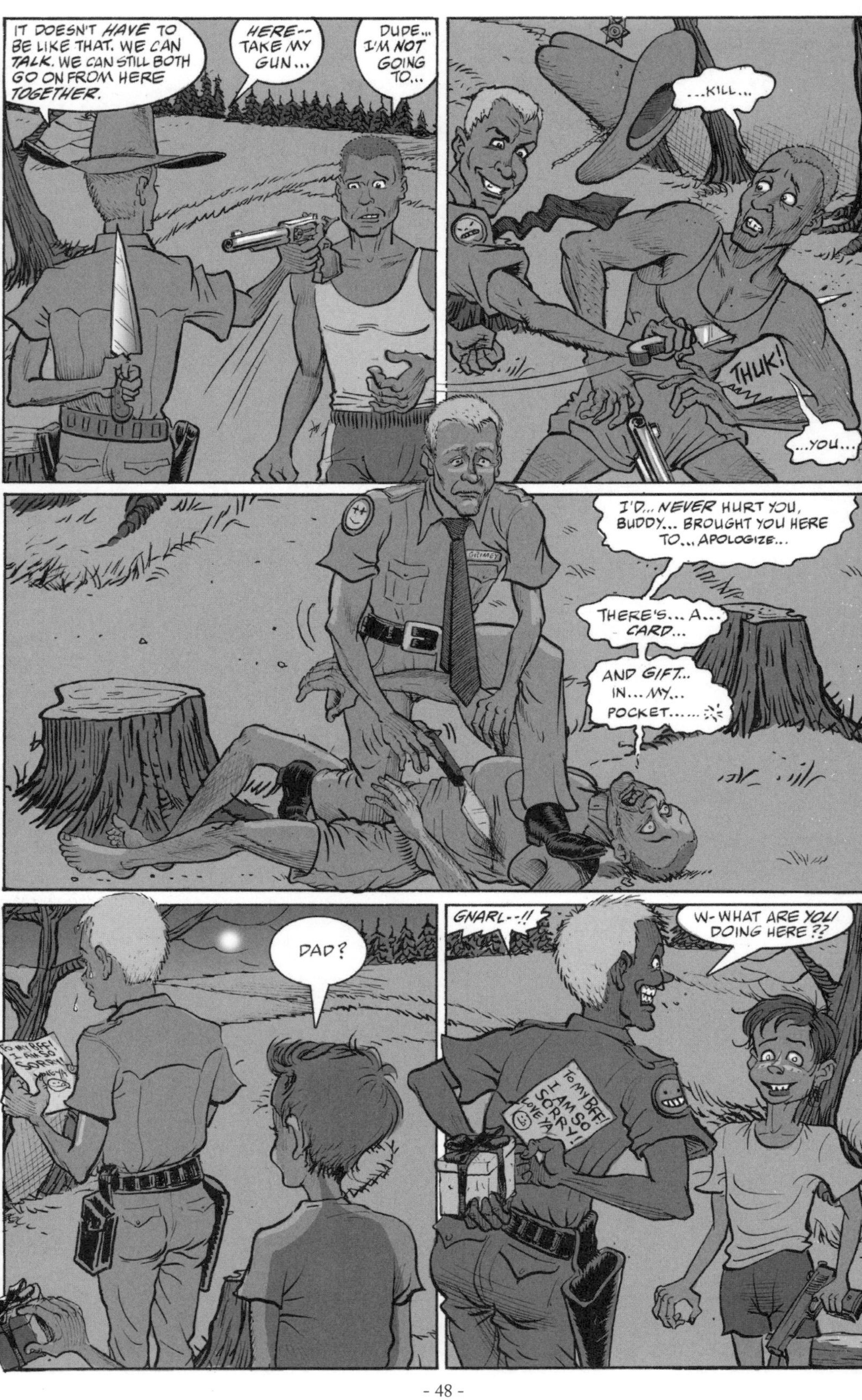
IT DOESN'T HAVE TO BE LIKE THAT. WE CAN TALK. WE CAN STILL BOTH GO ON FROM HERE TOGETHER.
HERE-- TAKE MY GUN...
DUDE... I'M NOT GOING TO...
...KILL...
THUK!
...YOU...
I'D... NEVER HURT YOU, BUDDY... BROUGHT YOU HERE TO... APOLOGIZE...
THERE'S... A... CARD...
AND GIFT... IN... MY... POCKET......
GRIMEY
TO MY BFF! I AM SO SORRY! LOVE YA
DAD?
GNARL--!!
W-WHAT ARE YOU DOING HERE??
TO MY BFF! I AM SO SORRY! LOVE YA

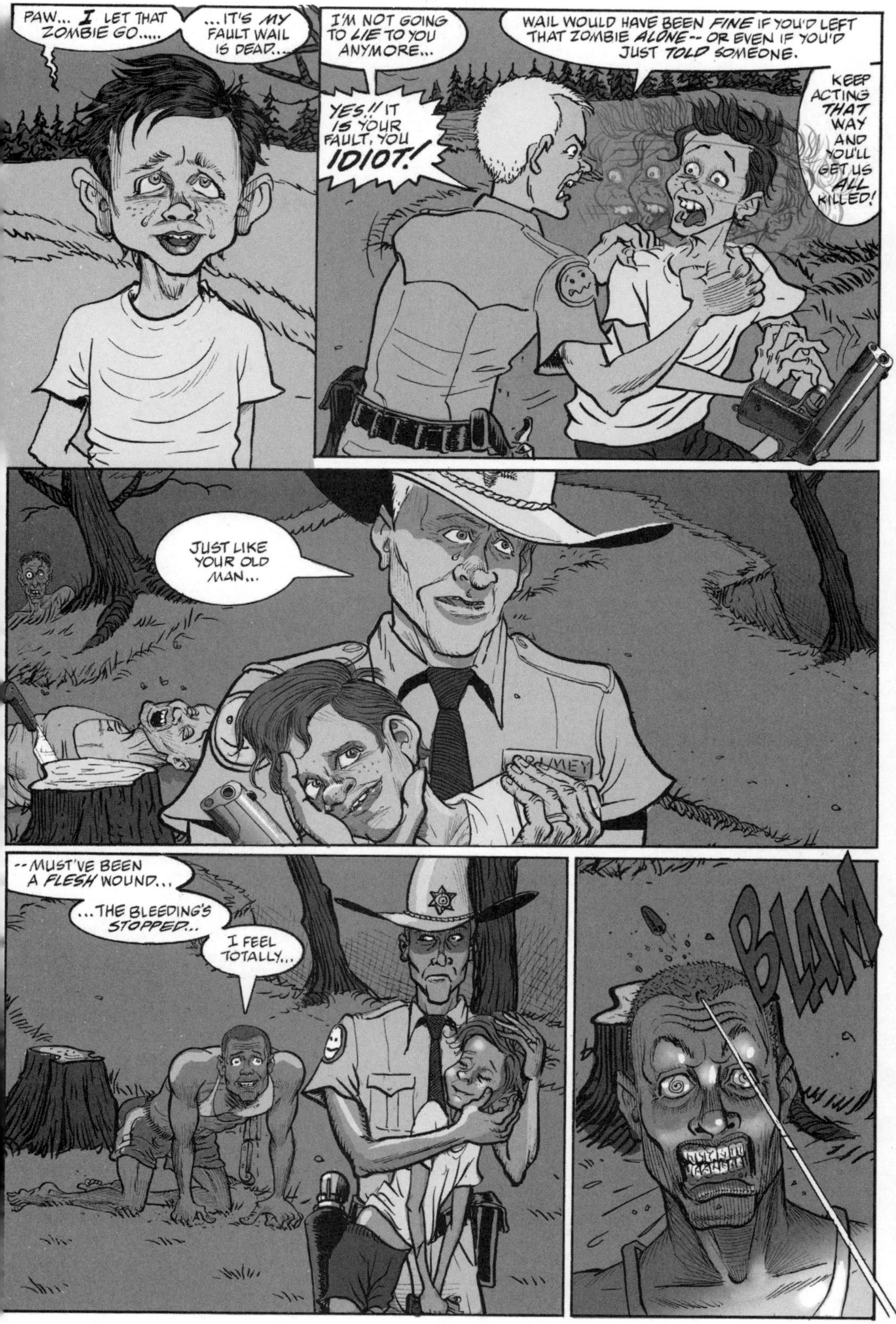
PAW... I LET THAT ZOMBIE GO.....
...IT'S MY FAULT WAIL IS DEAD...
I'M NOT GOING TO LIE TO YOU ANYMORE...
YES!! IT IS YOUR FAULT, YOU IDIOT!
WAIL WOULD HAVE BEEN FINE IF YOU'D LEFT THAT ZOMBIE ALONE-- OR EVEN IF YOU'D JUST TOLD SOMEONE.
KEEP ACTING THAT WAY AND YOU'LL GET US ALL KILLED!
JUST LIKE YOUR OLD MAN...
--MUST'VE BEEN A FLESH WOUND...
...THE BLEEDING'S STOPPED...
I FEEL TOTALLY...
BLAM

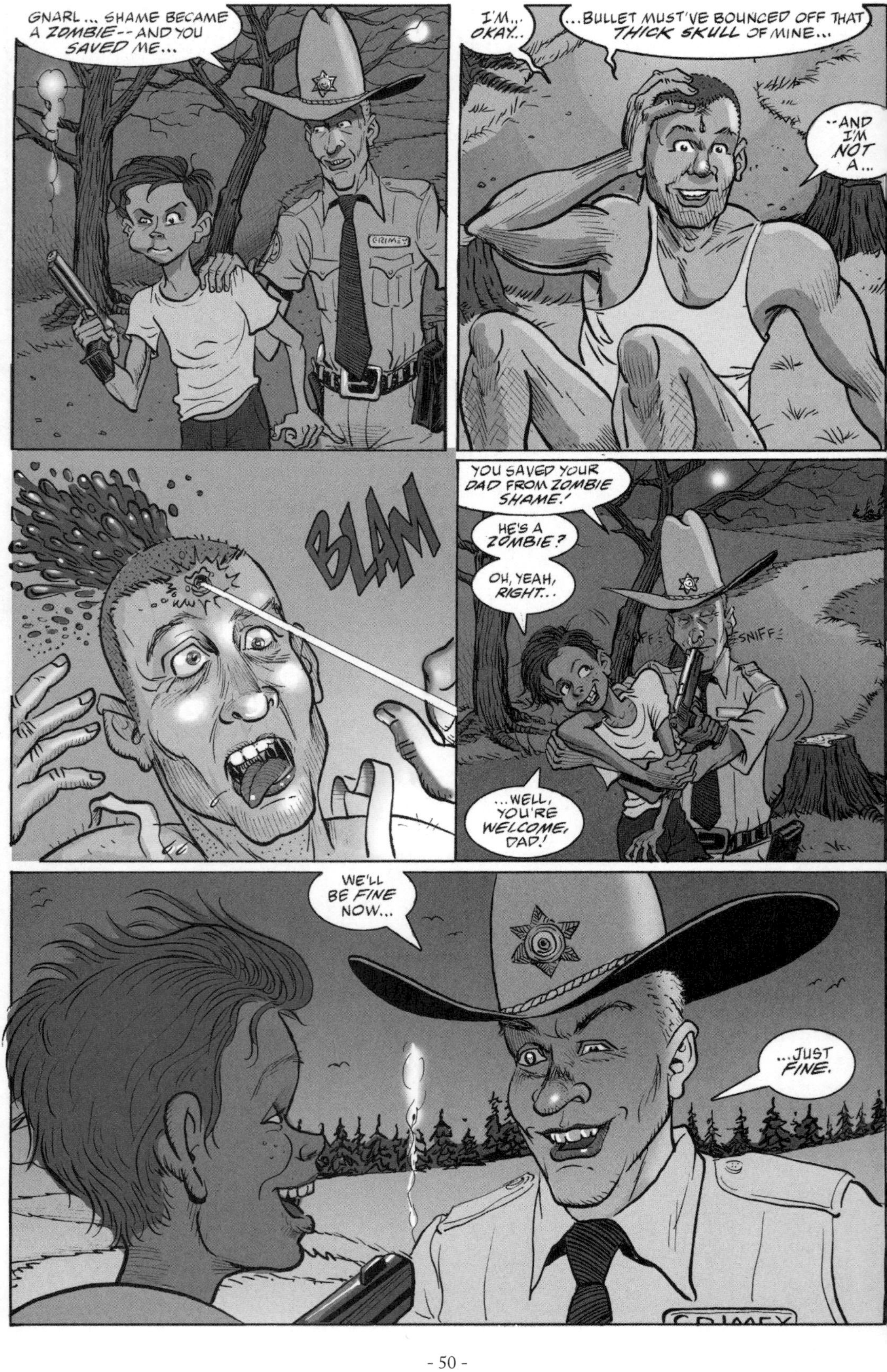
GNARL ... SHAME BECAME A ZOMBIE-- AND YOU SAVED ME...
CRIMEY
I'M... OKAY...
...BULLET MUST'VE BOUNCED OFF THAT THICK SKULL OF MINE...
--AND I'M NOT A...
BLAM
YOU SAVED YOUR DAD FROM ZOMBIE SHAME!
HE'S A ZOMBIE?
OH, YEAH, RIGHT...
SNIFF
...WELL, YOU'RE WELCOME, DAD!
WE'LL BE FINE NOW...
...JUST FINE.

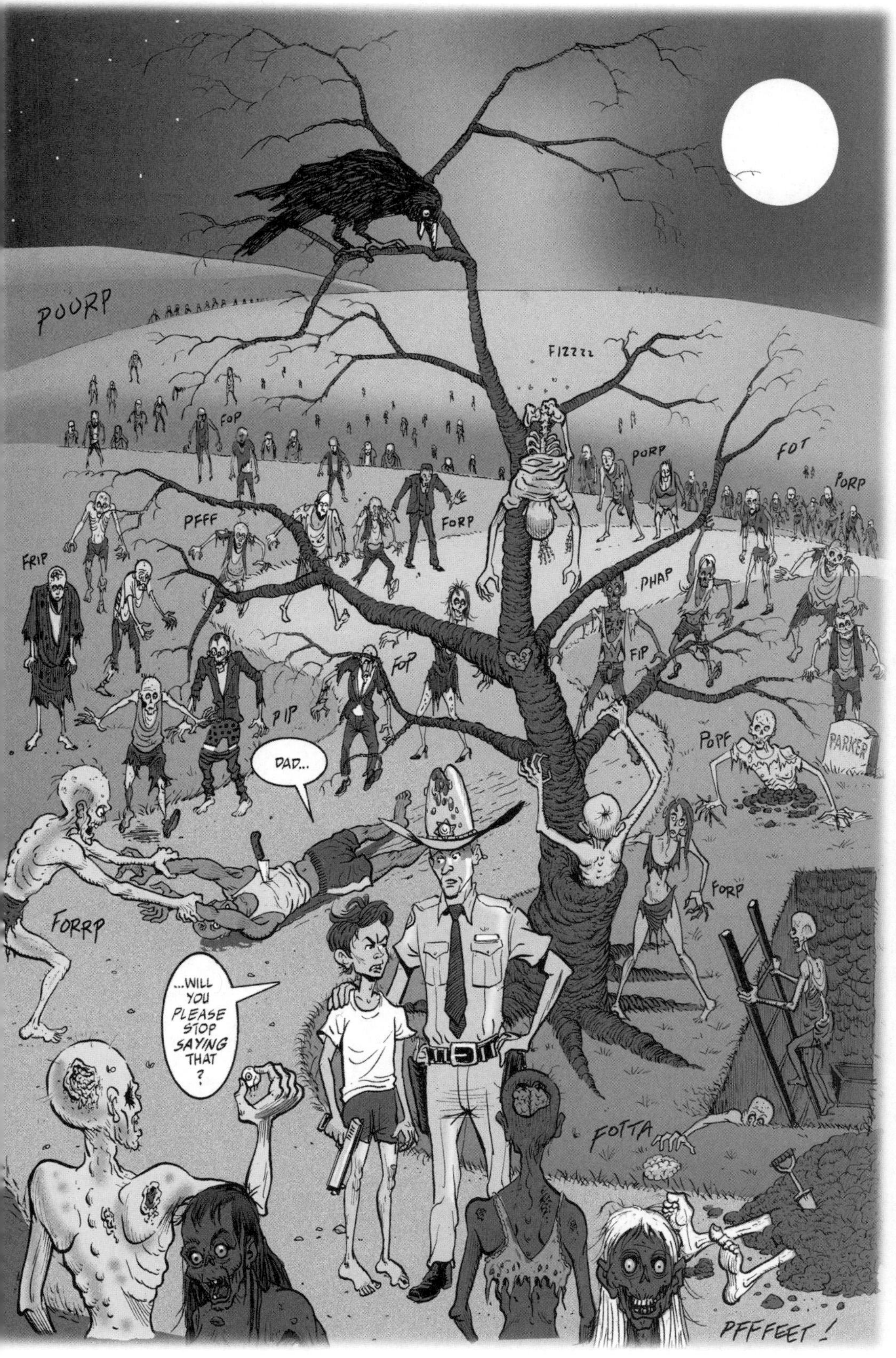
POORP
FIZZZZ
FOP
PORP
FOT
PORP
PFFF
FORP
FRIP
PHAP
FOP
FIP
PIP
POPF
PARKER
DAD...
FORP
FORRP
...WILL YOU PLEASE STOP SAYING THAT?
FOTTA
PFFFEET!

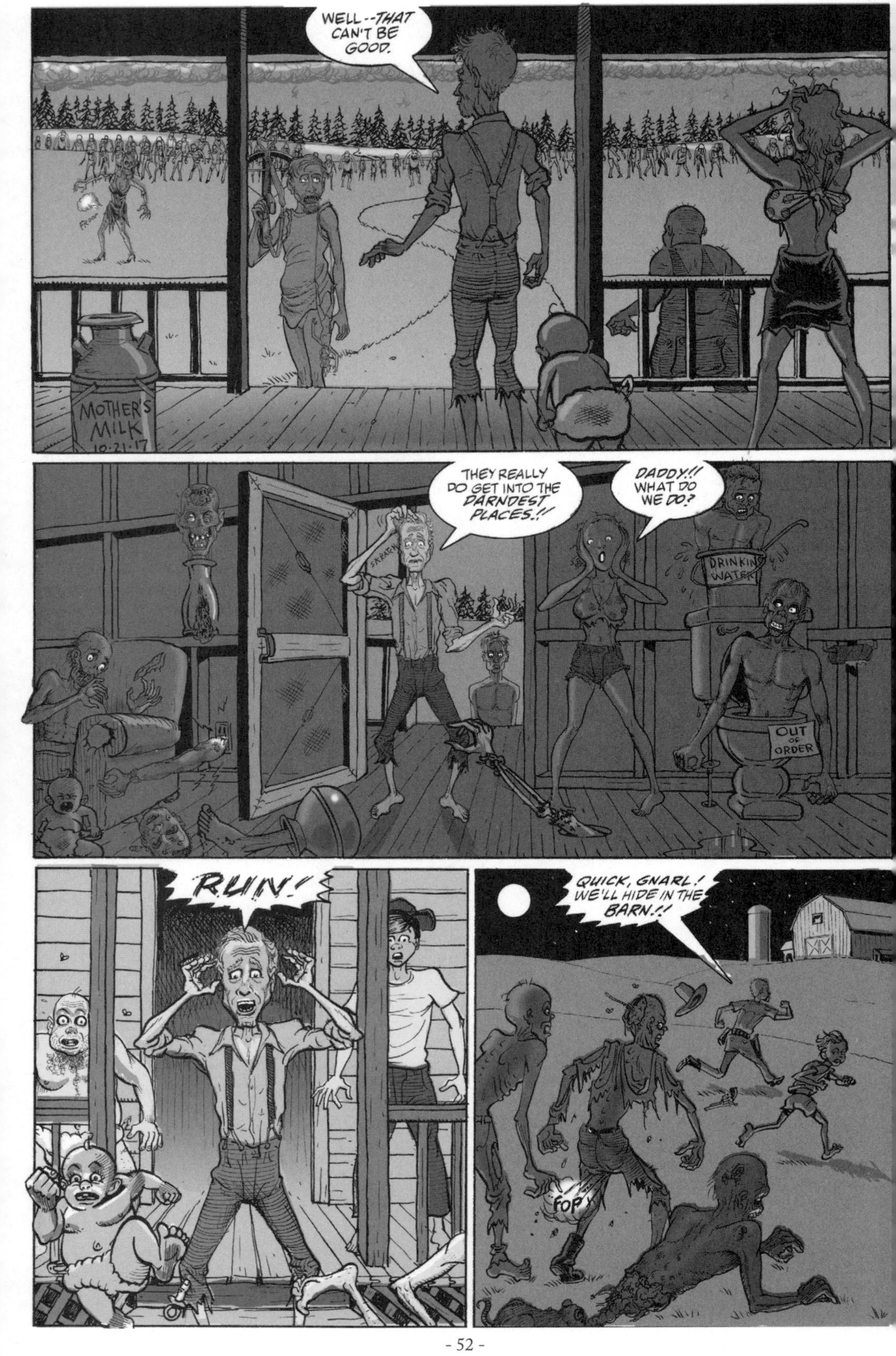
WELL --THAT CAN'T BE GOOD.
MOTHER'S MILK 10-21-17
THEY REALLY DO GET INTO THE DARNDEST PLACES.!!
DADDY!! WHAT DO WE DO?
DRINKIN WATE
OUT of ORDER
RUN!
QUICK, GNARL.! WE'LL HIDE IN THE BARN.!!
FOP

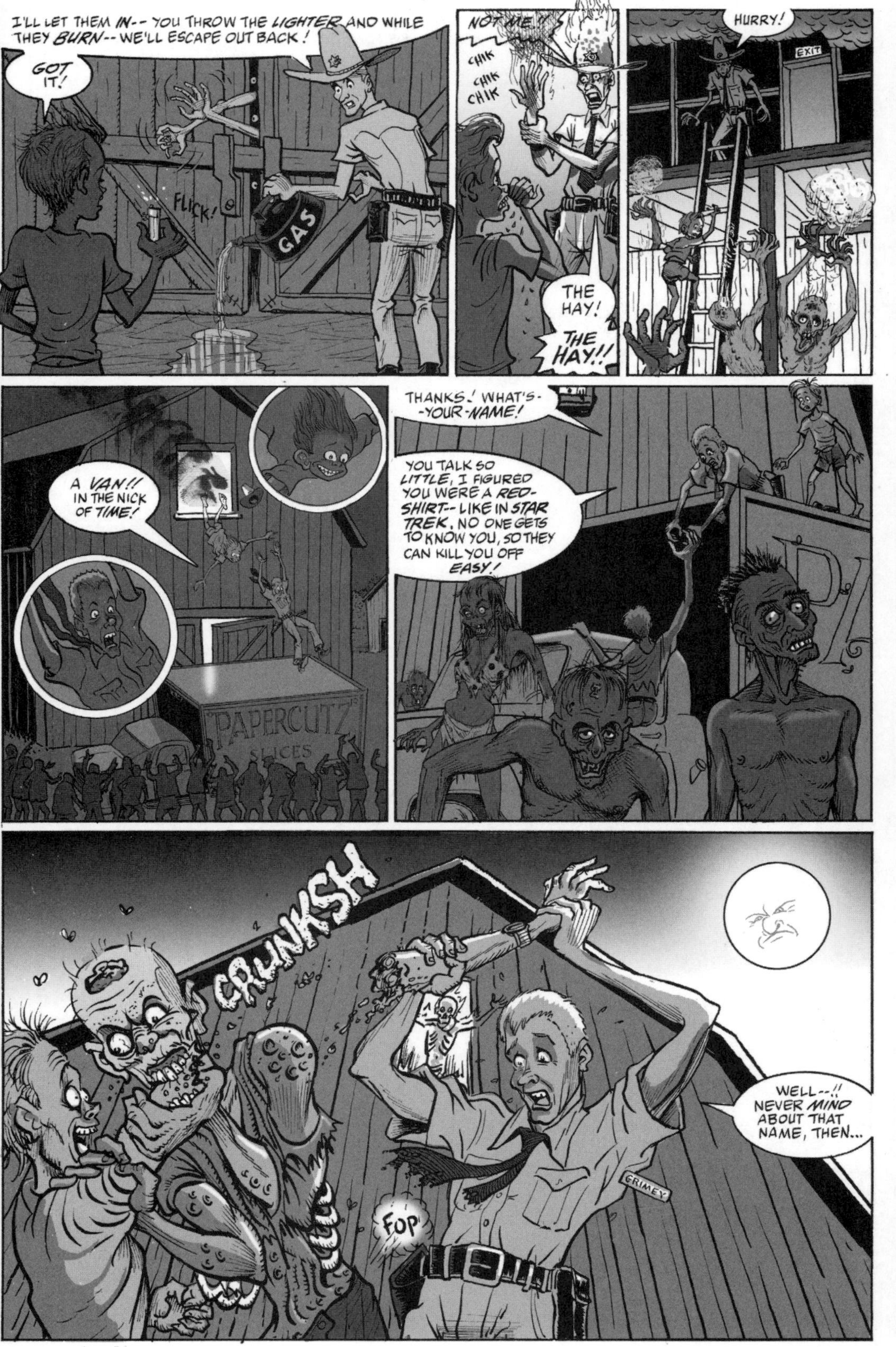
I'LL LET THEM IN-- YOU THROW THE LIGHTER AND WHILE THEY BURN-- WE'LL ESCAPE OUT BACK!
GOT IT!
FLICK!
GAS
NOT ME!
CHIK CHIK CHIK
THE HAY!
THE HAY!!
HURRY!
EXIT
A VAN!! IN THE NICK OF TIME!
PAPERCUTZ
SLICES
THANKS! WHAT'S-YOUR-NAME!
YOU TALK SO LITTLE, I FIGURED YOU WERE A RED-SHIRT-- LIKE IN STAR TREK, NO ONE GETS TO KNOW YOU, SO THEY CAN KILL YOU OFF EASY!
CRUNKSH
WELL--!! NEVER MIND ABOUT THAT NAME, THEN...
GRIMEY
FOP

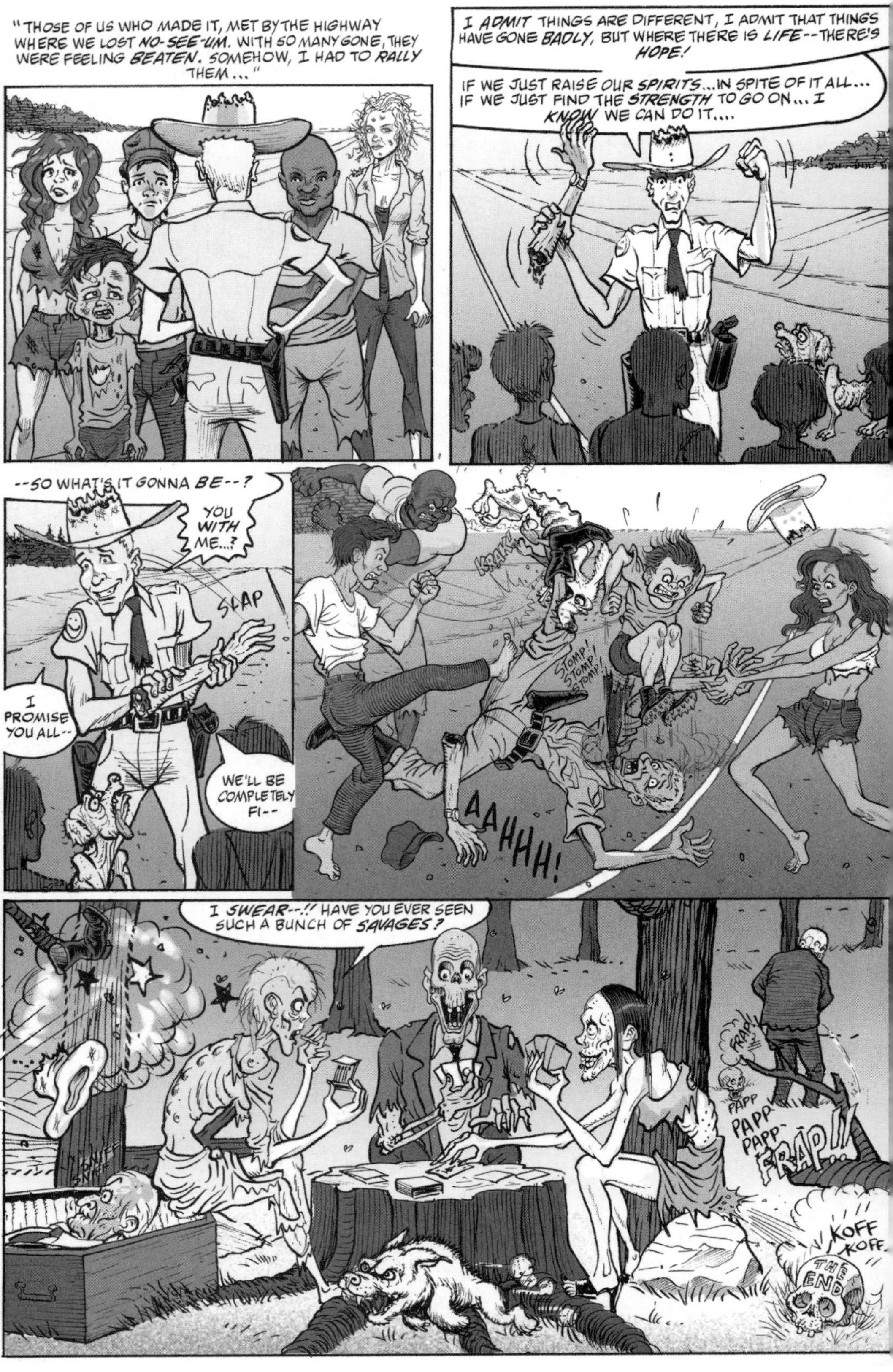
"THOSE OF US WHO MADE IT, MET BY THE HIGHWAY WHERE WE LOST NO-SEE-UM. WITH SO MANY GONE, THEY WERE FEELING BEATEN. SOMEHOW, I HAD TO RALLY THEM..."
I ADMIT THINGS ARE DIFFERENT, I ADMIT THAT THINGS HAVE GONE BADLY, BUT WHERE THERE IS LIFE--THERE'S HOPE!
IF WE JUST RAISE OUR SPIRITS... IN SPITE OF IT ALL... IF WE JUST FIND THE STRENGTH TO GO ON... I KNOW WE CAN DO IT....
--SO WHAT'S IT GONNA BE--?
YOU WITH ME...?
SLAP
I PROMISE YOU ALL--
WE'LL BE COMPLETELY FI--
KRAK!
STOMP! STOMP! STOMP!
AAHHHH!
I SWEAR--!! HAVE YOU EVER SEEN SUCH A BUNCH OF SAVAGES?
SNIFF SNIFF
FRAP!
PAPP
PAPP
PAPP-
FRAP!!...
KOFF KOFF
THE END

WATCH OUT FOR PAPERCUTZ™

Welcome to the fear-fraught fifth PAPERCUTZ SLICES graphic novel, the parody graphic novel series that died and came back to life, albeit looking a bit less colorful! I'm Jim Salicrup, Editor-in-Chief and erstwhile Supreme Marvel Zombie.

Here's a true story. One summer, when I was very young, my best friend invited me to spend a week or so with him, his mom, and his sister, at a lake house off somewhere in New Jersey. My parents, happy to be rid of me for a week, readily gave permission. So, off we all went to some unpronounceable lake in NJ! We stayed in a lovely vacation house on a hill that my friend's family were sharing with other folks, and on the lake, there was a boathouse. There was a shallow area beside the boathouse where we could play in the water, but we were warned if we went out beyond the boathouse there was a sudden twenty foot drop.

Did I mention that I don't know how to swim? Well, I didn't. But when you're very young you have no sense of your own mortality. I just loved lying on this Styrofoam surfboard they had and floating on the water in the big beautiful lake! It was the perfect way to spend a lazy summer day or seven. One day, as I was about to hop on the surfboard, it somehow slipped away from my grasp, and reaching for it, I slipped into deeper water. Fortunately, it wasn't the dreaded twenty-foot drop—I wasn't that insane! But even though I was a tall kid, the water was over my head, and, as I'm sure you recall, I can't swim.

Crazy thoughts go through your mind when you realize you're about to die. The craziest was that I thought if I drowned, my parents would never let me go on any more trips with my best friend. Uh… duh! As I was unsuccessfully trying to climb back on shore, unable to surmount the slime-covered concrete embankment at the water's edge —I remembered everything I ever heard about how to swim or float. Try as I may, none of it worked. I was doomed.

My best friend, floating nearby on an inflatable rubber raft, thought "Oh, that silly Jim! Look at him pretending to drown. Is there nothing he won't do for a gag?" But when he realized I was underwater longer than even an Olympic swimmer could probably hold his breath, he became concerned and paddled over to where I was drowning. With his help, I was able to pull myself up onto his raft. Gasping for air, I was rescued!

And that's the story of how Stefan Petrucha saved my life. Thanks, Stefan. I really do appreciate it!

Jim

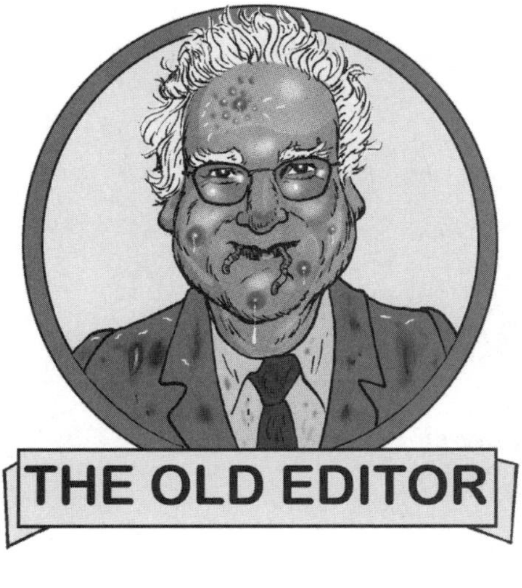
THE OLD EDITOR

STAY IN TOUCH!

EMAIL: salicrup@papercutz.com
WEB: www.papercutz.com
TWITTER: @papercutzgn
FACEBOOK: PAPERCUTZGRAPHICNOVELS
SNAIL MAIL: Papercutz, 160 Broadway,
Suite 700, East Wing,
New York, NY 10038

TALES FROM THE SCRIPT

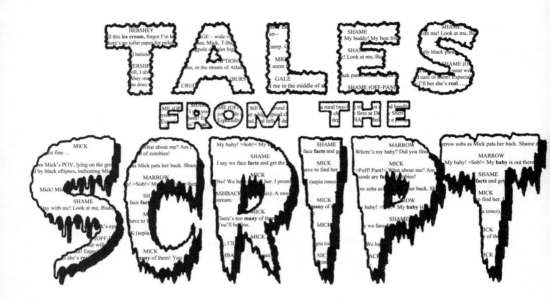

With this volume of PAPERCUTZ SLICES, the world-best-selling (and worst smelling*) parody graphic novel series, we decided to offer a new SPECIAL FEATURE. Just like DVDs of your favorite movies or TV series have special features, such as a voiceover track where you can hear the director or screenwriter or cast members tell you how brilliant they are, or what they had for lunch that day, we decided to try something a little different. Presented on the following pages are the actual SCRIPT pages created by writer Stefan Petrucha. Now you can see for yourself, exactly what artist Rick Parker was working from.

Page Five (Continued)

Panel 4: Gnarl stops short as he turns a tent corner and surprises GORY, his mom (see ref), and SHAME, who were obviously hugging and kissing before Gnarl spotted them. The boy is completely disgusted.

GNARL
Ew! That's so **gross**!

GORY
Ah!

SHAME
Ah!

Panel 5: Shame and Gory have pulled away from each other. As they straighten their clothes, Gnarl eyes them curiously.

GNARL
So, is my **dad** even still **alive**?

SHAME
'Course he is! He's a **tough** guy, and **smart**. Why, I tried killing him ten, twenty times!

Page Six (Continued)

Panel 5: Shame kneels next to Gnarl as well.

SHAME
Listen to your mom, little man, and to **me**, too.

SHAME
Since your dad's not here, I think of you as **mine**. Always wanted a talking pet.

GNARL
Yes, Shame.

Page Seven (Continued)

Panel 4: Mick stumbles onto the graveyard scene from Night of the Living Dead with Barbara and Jimmy. Their zombie is visible in the background. (see ref)

CAPTION
"Whatever **happened**, I had to hold on to my humanity. I would **not** become one of those men who **refuse** to ask directions."

MICK
Excuse, me, but…

JIMMY
They're coming to get you, **Barbara**, there's one of them now!

Panel 5: As the zombie takes a bite out of Jimmy's shoulder, Jimmy points to the left for Mick.

JIMMY
I heard there was a camp of survivors up on that hill!

MICK
Thank you kindly. Say, buddy, does that really taste like chicken?

ZOMBIE
Eh.

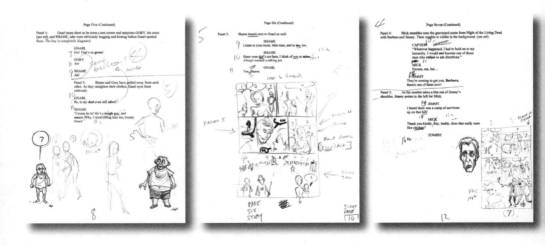

*Yeah, we used the same joke on the back cover. What? Don't you believe in recycling?

Panel 1: A grassy hill near a rural two-lane road. An armed bandit has just emerged from a flipped pickup truck after a high speed chase. He fires at Deputy Sheriff MICK GRIMEY, hitting him in the gut. Mick's pal, and fellow deputy, SHAME, holding a pump-shotgun, stares at Mick shocked.

SFX (GUN)
Blam

SHAME (BURST)
Mick!

Panel 2: Though staggered, Mick shoots the bad guy.

SFX (GUN)
Pow

MICK
He hit me in the vest. I'll be fine, **Shame**…

Panel 3: A second gun-toting bad guy, having appeared from passenger side of the flipped pickup, shoots Mick. We see the bullet enter one side of Mick's abdomen, and exit from his back.

SFX (GUN)
Boom

MICK
…just fine …

Panel 4: From Mick's POV, lying on the ground, we look up at a worried Shame. The panel is bordered by black ellipses, indicating Mick is closing his eyes.

SHAME
Mick! Mick! My buddy! My best friend!

SHAME
Stay with me! Look at me, Buddy!

Panel 5: A completely black panel. Mick's eyes are closed.

SHAME (OFF-PANEL)
If you die can I get your wife and kid? I **promise** I'll take good care of them! Especially that **hot** little wife of yours, why I'll bet she's **real**….

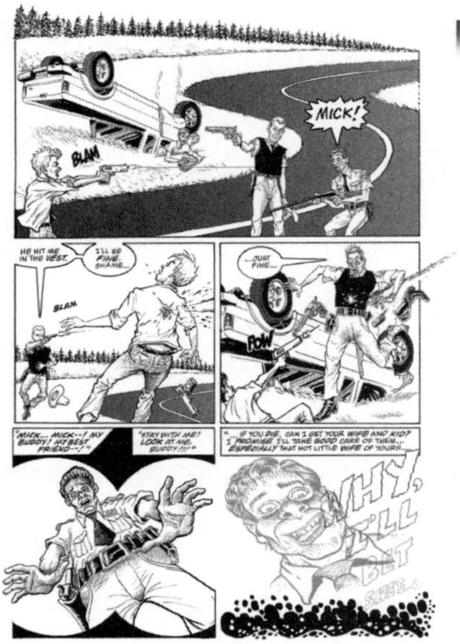
BLAM
MICK!
HE HIT ME IN THE VEST.
I'LL BE FINE, SHAME...
BLAM
...JUST FINE...
POW
"MICK... MICK--! MY BUDDY! MY BEST FRIEND--!"
"STAY WITH ME! LOOK AT ME, BUDDY!!!"
"...IF YOU DIE, CAN I GET YOUR WIFE AND KID? I PROMISE I'LL TAKE GOOD CARE OF THEM... ESPECIALLY THAT HOT LITTLE WIFE OF YOURS...
WHY, I'LL BET

Page Eight

Panel 1: At camp, the zombies have been defeated. A bunch of zombie bodies have amusing things sticking out of their heads, like forks. As the others try to clean up, Gale berates them. Shame and Gory are notably missing.

CAPTION
Back at camp…

GALE
Have we **already** forgotten who we are? Do we **not clean up** after ourselves anymore?

GALE
I can't remember the last time I heard a **please** or a **thank-you** or even an--

Panel 2: Mick steps into camp. Gale screams at him.

MICK
Excuse me. I seem to have misplaced my family.

GALE
You interrupt me in the middle of a sentence again, I **swear** I'll bite out your eyeballs!

Panel 3: A hair-mussed Gory and Gnarl embrace Mick. In the background, Shame pulls up his pants.

GNARL (BURST)
Dad!

GORY
You're **alive**!

SHAME
That's great. Just… **great**.

Panel 4: Mick addresses a group of the survivors, including Wail, Gory, Shame, the blonde San Andreas, the little girl No-see-um, her mom, Marrow, the bigoted Burl and the bald, African American T-Bagg.

MICK
The way I see it, if we're going to survive this thing, we need **supplies** – batteries, corn dogs, pork rinds and, maybe if we're lucky, toilet paper.

MICK
T-Bagg, **Merle**, you come with me. We're heading into the city!

GORY
But you just got here!

MICK
Don't worry, honey. I'll be **fine**.

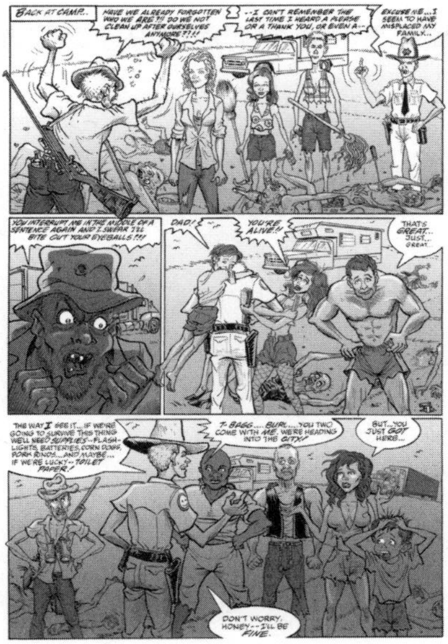

BACK AT CAMP..
HAVE WE ALREADY FORGOTTEN WHO WE ARE?!! DO WE NOT CLEAN UP AFTER OURSELVES ANYMORE??!!
--I CAN'T REMEMBER THE LAST TIME I HEARD A PLEASE OR A THANK YOU, OR EVEN A--
EXCUSE ME...I SEEM TO HAVE MISPLACED MY FAMILY...
YOU INTERRUPT ME IN THE MIDDLE OF A SENTENCE AGAIN AND I SWEAR I'LL BITE OUT YOUR EYEBALLS!?!
DAD!
YOU'RE ALIVE!!
THAT'S GREAT... JUST... GREAT...
THE WAY I SEE IT... IF WE'RE GOING TO SURVIVE THIS THING WE'LL NEED SUPPLIES--FLASH-LIGHTS, BATTERIES, CORN DOGS, PORK RINDS... AND MAYBE... IF WE'RE LUCKY--TOILET PAPER!
T-BAGG.... BURL.... YOU TWO COME WITH ME. WE'RE HEADING INTO THE CITY!
BUT... YOU JUST GOT HERE...
DON'T WORRY, HONEY--I'LL BE FINE.

Page Nine

Panel 1: SPLASH PAGE – wide view of a huge city block swarming (and I mean SWARMING) with Zombies. Mick, T-Bagg and Burl are pinned on the roof of a van parked near a tall building. A flagpole dangles high above them.

CAPTION
Soon, in the streets of Atlanta…

MICK (BURST)
CRUD!

SFX:

FRIPP FRAPP FIP FROOOP PROPP-A M-PROOPA

SOON, IN THE STREETS OF ATLANTA....
CRUD!
FRAPP
FRIPP
M-PROPPA
PROPP-A
FROOOP
FIP

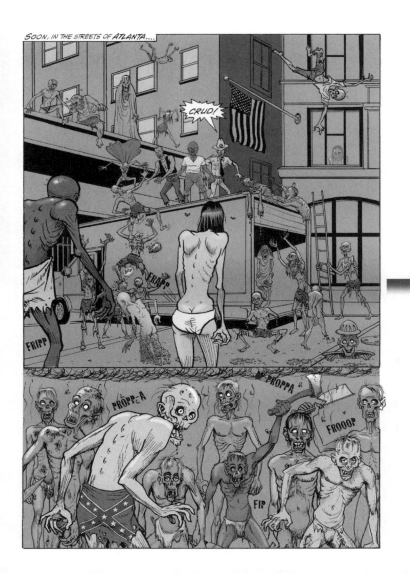

Panel 1: As the sound rises, Mick waves for everyone to get under a car. Gory hides with Marrow. Gnarl hides with zombie No-see-um.

SOUND (LOUDER)
Beep Beep Beep

MICK (WHISPER)
Everyone crawl under a car to **hide**!

Panel 2: Tight shot of Mick under a car, sweating.

MICK (WHISPER)
Stay **completely** silent!

SFX
Beep

Panel 3: Tight shot of Gnarl and No-see-um under a different car. No-see-um tries to nibble on him.

GNARL (WHISPER)
Quiet!

SFX
Beep Beep Beeep Poot

Panel 4: Tight shot of Marrow and Gory under a car. Marrow, seeing her daughter off-panel, is panicked, hand to mouth.

MARROW (WHISPER)
My little girl!

SFX

POOT BEEP BEEP

Panel 5: Gory has grabbed Marrow's mouth to keep her quiet as the wheels of a tiny Shriner car roll right by them. All we see at this point is the wheels.

SOUND
Beep Beep Beep Beep

BEEP
BEEP
QUICK, EVERYONE--!! CRAWL UNDER A CAR TO HIDE!
BEEP
BEEP
BEEP
EVERYONE STAY COMPLETELY SILENT!
BEEP
BEEP
POOT!
BEEP
BEEP
BEEP
QUIET!
QUIET!
MY LITTLE GIRL!
POOT!
BEEP
BEEP
BEEP
BEEP
BEEP
BEEP

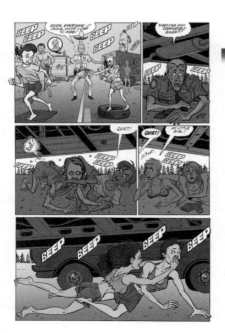

Panel 1: An overhead shot reveals zombie Shriners, wearing fezzes, driving their little cars past the hiding survivors.

CAPTION
"We'd seen **terrible** things, but none so awful as the zombie Shriners."

SFX
Beep Beep Beep Beep

Panel 2: Beneath his car, Gnarl pushes zombie No-see-um out.

GNARL (WHISPER)
Quit trying to **bite** me!

SFX
POOPT FAA-POPF

Panel 3: The Shriners drive off. No-see-um rushes off into the woods near the interstate. Marrow, panicked, calls after her.

MARROW
My baby!

Panel 4: The Shriners gone, the survivors look at the woods.

GNARL
Is it **my** fault No-see-um is gone, even though I shoved her out there?

GORY
Of course not.

MICK
Everyone stay here. **I'll** go after her.

Panel 5: A worried Gory looks at a somber Mick.

GORY
You're running off again?

MICK
Don't worry, I'll be **fine**.

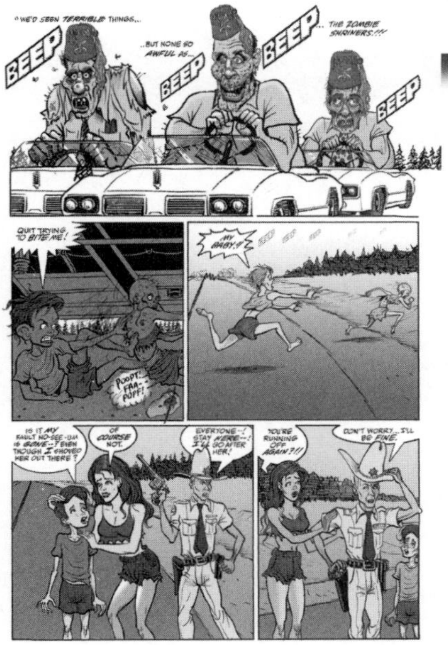
"WE'D SEEN TERRIBLE THINGS...
BEEP
...BUT NONE SO AWFUL AS...
BEEP
BEEP
... THE ZOMBIE SHRINERS.!!"
BEEP
QUIT TRYING TO BITE ME!
POOPT! FAA--POPF!
MY BABY!!
IS IT MY FAULT NO-SEE-UM IS GONE--? EVEN THOUGH I SHOVED HER OUT THERE?
OF COURSE NOT.
EVERYONE--! STAY HERE--! I'LL GO AFTER HER!
YOU'RE RUNNING OFF AGAIN?!!
DON'T WORRY... I'LL BE FINE.

Panel 1: Switch to the woods. Mick is running full tilt from a mob of zombies.

CAPTION
Shortly…

MICK
@#$%!

SFX
Frip Fopp

Panel 2: Mick rushes out of the forest back to the interstate. Gory, Marrow and the others wait.

MARROW
Where's my baby? Did you find her?

MICK
>Puff! Pant!< What about me? Am I **chopped liver**? The woods are **full** of zombies!

Panel 3: Marrow sobs as Mick pats her back. Shame shakes his head.

MARROW
My baby! >Sob!< My **baby** is out there!

SHAME
I say we face **facts** and get the **heck** out of here!

MICK
No! We have to find her. I promised.

Panel 4: FLASHBACK (sepia tones). A sweating Mick leaves the zombie No-see-um in small hollow by a stream.

MICK
There's too **many** of them! You stay here, No-see-um! You'll be fine.

MICK
Me, I'll just…

Panel 5: FLASHBACK (sepia tones). Mick runs full tilt from the hidden child.

NICK
Be back later! Promise!

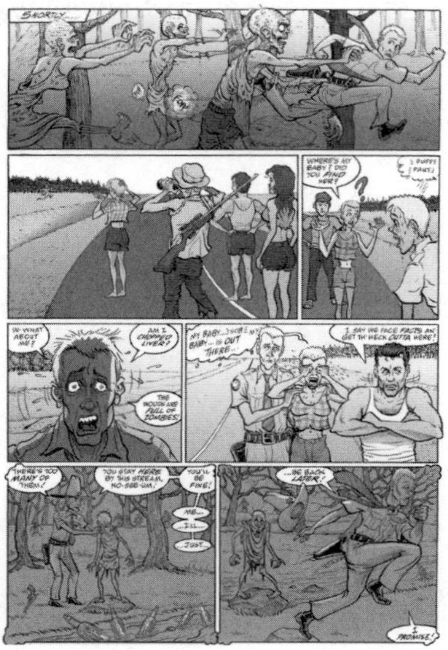
WHERE'S MY BABY? DID YOU FIND HER?
W-WHAT ABOUT ME?
AM I CHOPPED LIVER?
THE WOODS ARE FULL OF ZOMBIES!
MY BABY... IS OUT THERE...
I SAY WE FACE FACTS AN' GET TH' HECK OUTTA HERE!
THERE'S TOO MANY OF THEM!
YOU STAY HERE BY THIS STREAM, NO-SEE-UM!
YOU'LL BE FINE!
ME...
...I'LL...
...JUST...
...BE BACK LATER!
I PROMISE!

Page Thirty-three

Panel 1: Inside a darkened ice cream parlor, Hershey sits at a bar in foreground, mouth covered with fudge, empty sundae glasses piled high. In the background, Mick and Penn enter from the front door.

MICK
Naggie said we might find you here. You okay?

HERSHEY
I feel like such an old **fool**, Mick.

HERSHEY
Ate all this **ice cream,** forgot I'm **lactose intolerant** and that there's no toilet paper for miles.

Panel 2: Mick and Penn stand behind Hershey, who lowers his head in shame.

HERSHEY
And the barn, well, I always **knew** they were dead, but I liked the **sound** they made – reminded me of cattle **looing**. What kind of man does that make me?

MICK
A man who likes the sound of cattle.

HERSHEY
That's kind of you, Mick. Kind of **crazy**, actually, but, Ah **appreciate** it.

Panel 3: As darkness settles outside, Penn nervously points toward the door. Mick shakes his head.

PENN
Should we head back?

MICK
It's getting **dark**. We'll be **fine** here until morning.

Panel 4: Close-up of a panicking Penn.

PENN
No! No! Do **NOT** say we'll be fine!

PENN
Whenever you say that…

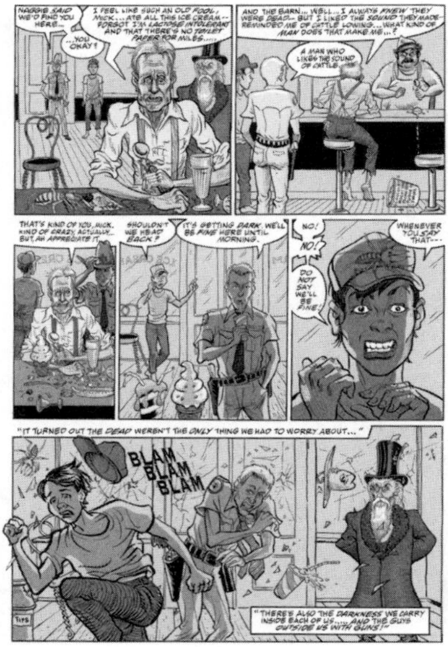
NAGGIE SAID WE'D FIND YOU HERE...
...YOU OKAY?
I FEEL LIKE SUCH AN OLD FOOL, MICK... ATE ALL THIS ICE CREAM-- FORGOT I'M LACTOSE INTOLERANT AND THAT THERE'S NO TOILET PAPER FOR MILES....
AND THE BARN... WELL... I ALWAYS KNEW THEY WERE DEAD-- BUT I LIKED THE SOUND THEY MADE-- REMINDED ME OF CATTLE LOWING... WHAT KIND OF MAN DOES THAT MAKE ME...?
A MAN WHO LIKES THE SOUND OF CATTLE.
THAT'S KIND OF YOU, MICK. KIND OF CRAZY, ACTUALLY... BUT, AH APPRECIATE IT.
SHOULDN'T WE HEAD BACK?
IT'S GETTING DARK. WE'LL BE FINE HERE UNTIL MORNING.
NO!
NO!
DO NOT SAY WE'LL BE FINE!
WHENEVER YOU SAY THAT---
"IT TURNED OUT THE DEAD WEREN'T THE ONLY THING WE HAD TO WORRY ABOUT..."
BLAM
BLAM
BLAM
"THERE'S ALSO THE DARKNESS WE CARRY INSIDE EACH OF US..... AND THE GUYS OUTSIDE US WITH GUNS!"

Panel 5: Penn ducks as the windows are shattered by gunfire.

CAPTION
"It turned out the **dead** weren't the only thing we had to worry about."

SOUND (GUNFIRE)
Blam Blam

CAPTION
"There's also the darkness we carry **inside** each of us. And the guys **outside** us with guns."

Panel 1: On the porch of the farmhouse, the other survivors see the hordes of zombies coming.

HERSHEY
Well, **that** can't be good.

Panel 2: The survivors look back inside the house to see zombies crawling out from all sorts of small spaces – beneath the couch, out of a flower vase, from a lamp, etc.

HERSHEY
They really do get into the **darndest** places.

NAGGIE
Daddy, what do we do?

Panel 3: Hershey screams as the survivors bolt from the farmhouse.

HERSHEY (BURST)
RUN!

Panel 4: Mick and Gnarl race for the barn, the zombies hot on their trail.

MICK
Inside, Gnarl!

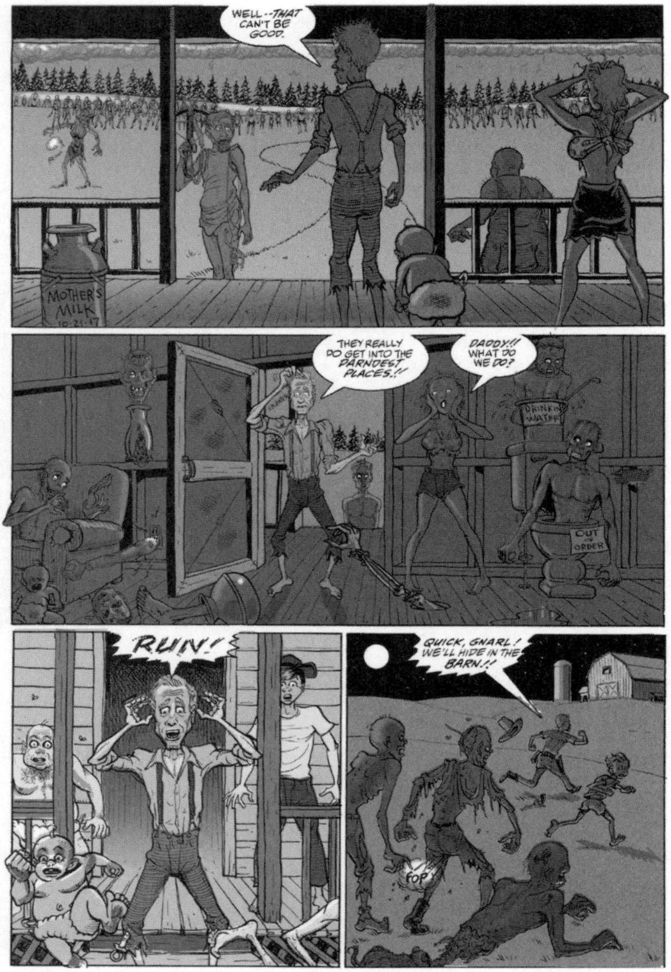
WELL--THAT CAN'T BE GOOD.
MOTHER'S MILK 10-21-17
THEY REALLY DO GET INTO THE DARNDEST PLACES.!!
DADDY!! WHAT DO WE DO?
DRINKIN WATER
OUT OF ORDER
RUN!
QUICK, GNARL! WE'LL HIDE IN THE BARN.!!
FOP